VILLAGE

VILLAGE

As It Happened
Through a Fifteen Year Period
ROBERT MCALMON
EDITED WITH AN INTRODUCTION BY
Edward N. S. Lorusso
University of New Mexico Press
Albuquerque

Library of Congress Cataloging-in-Publication Data
McAlmon, Robert, 1896–1956.
 Village : as it happened through a fifteen-year period / Robert
McAlmon ; edited with an introduction by Edward N.S. Lorusso.
  p.   cm.
 Includes bibliographical references.
 ISBN 0-8263-1200-4
 I. Lorusso, Edward N. S.   II. Title.
PS3525.A1143V55   1990
813'.52—dc20   89-70638
                                                      CIP

Introduction

F ew prominent literary figures have made the transition from fame to oblivion as thoroughly as Robert McAlmon. His meteoric rise in 1920s Paris as publisher and writer was unequalled; his descent from grace to the deserts of the American Southwest was also unique. When his name does spark recognition among today's readers, it is usually as a social figure of the expatriate movement. McAlmon's name is mentioned in nearly all of the memoirs and biographies dealing with that era. He knew everybody, published many of the new voices of the decade, and (with varying degrees of success) was friends with many of the major literary figures.

McAlmon's reputation as a writer has so completely declined that he has become somewhat of a mystery man. Because few of his books have been published in the United States, it is difficult for modern readers to judge his merits. The publication of *Being Geniuses Together* in 1968 marked only the third McAlmon volume to be published in this country. In 1937 New Directions printed a volume of poetry, *Not Alone Lost*; and in 1963, a New York publisher reprinted *Distinguished Air* as *There Was a Rustle of Black Silk Stockings*. This reprint was an attempt to cash in on the sexual frankness of McAlmon's writing. Only his long poem

North America, Continent of Conjecture is currently available in a reprint edition.

Even so eminent a scholar as Hugh Kenner gets his facts confused when, in *The Pound Era*, he states that the Kansas-born McAlmon, "came to Paris from Nebraska, the inadvertent husband of a millionairess. He published his friends' books; also (1922) A *Hasty Bunch*, meaning stories he did not choose to revise because that would destroy their primal authenticity."

A *Hasty Bunch*, a collection of short stories, received several very good reviews and established McAlmon as a promising, if raw, writer, one who did not polish his prose style. Kenner's comments about the primal authenticity underline a basic concept of McAlmon's writing: that the style as well as the story should be honest, and that this gut reaction cannot be maintained through rewrites.

His next two books, *Post-Adolescence* (1923) and *Village* (1924), continued McAlmon's use of American English in a plain, rough style, and furthered his explorations of primal authenticity. *Village* in particular utilizes the American rhythm and vocabulary of its small-town characters. The loose construction of the novel, that is, its episodic structure, also complements the story line in its simplicity.

In her review of *Village*, Ethel Moorhead, poet and editor of *This Quarter*, said: "Robert McAlmon is not concerned with the parade of English as the English do it. He handles a sensible, robust, racy language convincingly. . . . No obstacle of English language in the way of ornament, clever paradox, and the like is allowed to spoil its purity."

Ezra Pound, who championed McAlmon's cause and tried to find an American publisher for his friend, said, "America is now teeming with printed books written by imitators of McAlmon, inferior to the original." Pound also wrote about the "honesty that divides say McAlmon from Sinclair Lewis, and makes the latter so acceptable to the boob."

Despite his supporters, McAlmon's possibly lazy theory was also applied to proofreading and editing. His books are filled with typos,

curious punctuation, and obvious inconsistencies. But these nega-
tive factors should not keep one from enjoying the brisk writing
style or the straightforward, unsentimental prose of McAlmon.

Another review praised *Village* for its sparseness: "It recalls
Sinclair Lewis' Gopher Prairie and Sherwood Anderson's Winesburg. There is the same isolation, the same type of shut-in
lives. . . . The pictures drawn by the author possess neither Sinclair Lewis' humor nor Sherwood Anderson's *chiaro-oscuro* [*sic*].
They are deliberately bare, with a thorough-going objectivity and
frankness, reminiscent of a pure, undiluted Maupassant."

McAlmon knew his subject well. He was born in Clifton,
Kansas, on 9 March 1896. His father was a minister, a Princeton
graduate, who traveled often and moved the family sporadically.
McAlmon spent much of his childhood in South Dakota and
Minnesota. It is perhaps this prairie childhood that was at the root
of his unabashed straightforwardness, which many found charming. Others found him blunt, rude, and offensive.

In 1920, while living in New York and working as an artist's
model, McAlmon met, through William Carlos Williams, the
English heiress Winifred Ellerman, who wrote under the name
Bryher. They agreed to marry and in February 1921 sailed to
Europe to honeymoon. This marriage is central to the slightly
smarmy reputation that McAlmon achieved. Many people assumed the marriage was strictly a business deal from which McAlmon got money and Bryher got her return from her family. The large
divorce settlement that McAlmon received earned him the nick-
name "McAlimony." Whatever private agreement they had, the
public result was that McAlmon was perceived to be an opportu-
nist. The fact that he spent his money freely on others and set
himself up as publisher did little to dispel the bad opinion of some.

McAlmon remained tight-lipped about his marriage. When
McAlmon's long-time friend and supporter, William Carlos Williams, bluntly stated that the marriage had remained unconsum-
mated, McAlmon quickly broke off relations with him. Others,
like Kay Boyle, believe that McAlmon was simply duped into the

marriage, which allowed Bryher to continue her affair with H. D. In any case, McAlmon seemed able to maintain a friendly relationship with both women. He published books for both Bryher and H. D. through his *Contact Magazine* and Contact Publishing Company.

McAlmon was indisputably the most important publisher in Paris, both in the number of books he published and in the range of material. McAlmon published Gertrude Stein's *The Making of Americans*; Ernest Hemingway's first major book, *Three Stories and Ten Poems*; Djuna Barnes's *Ladies Almanack*, an underground who's who of the lesbian colony in Paris; and Nathanael West's *The Dream Life of Balso Snell*. Through his *Contact Magazine*, co-edited by William Carlos Williams from December 1920 to Summer 1921, McAlmon published material by himself and Williams, but also by Pound, Mina Loy, Marsden Hartley, Wallace Stevens, Marianne Moore, Kay Boyle, and H. D. This "little magazine," established before he met Bryher, was supported through McAlmon's earnings as a model. It is interesting to note that the life of *Contact Magazine* roughly paralleled the "courtship," marriage, and sailing for Europe of McAlmon and Bryher, and lasted only until Contact Publishing was established.

McAlmon's support for other writers and artists was not limited to publishing their books. McAlmon gave financial aid to the ailing Italian poet Emanuel Carnevali; gave James Joyce a monthly allowance of $150 (as well as typing and proofreading sections of Joyce's *Ulysses*, no easy task); and picked up the tab for a trip to Spain with Hemingway. It was during this trip that Hemingway tried to win over McAlmon to the thrills of bullfighting. McAlmon resisted. McAlmon also disagreed with Hemingway's assertions concerning realism. During this trip they saw a maggot-infested dog lying dead on a railway flatcar. Hemingway was fascinated by the sight; McAlmon was not. Hemingway advised "a detached and scientific attitude. . . . We of our generation must inure ourselves to the sight of pain and grim reality." Hemingway continued,

"Hell, Mac, you write like a realist. Are you going to be a romantic on us?"

McAlmon was never a romantic. His writing was always considered terse, and his characters—homosexuals, lesbians, bohemians, Mexican peasants, Spanish Loyalists, migrant workers, hypocrites—were hardly the stuff of romanticism. It was just this willingness to take dead aim at his subject that caused James Joyce to dismiss McAlmon's *Being Geniuses Together* as "the office boy's revenge."

Because he spared no one in his volume of memoirs, many people, including Joyce, believed that McAlmon was striking back at everyone because of his ultimately failed career. But it should be remembered that McAlmon is as hard on himself in *Being Geniuses Together* as he is on anyone else:

> As we had decided to drink through the list of French drinks, Joyce began dropping his cigars. At first I leaned to pick them up and return them to him. When I could no longer lean without falling on my face I took to lighting the cigars and handing them to him.

McAlmon never attempts to paint a picture of himself as saint, nor does he gossip about the carousing activities of others without duly including himself in the picture.

Joyce's castigation of McAlmon was particularly hard to take. After all, McAlmon had been supporting Joyce for quite a while and had been a regular drinking buddy. McAlmon was more than just a social acquaintance, however. He sought subscriptions for Joyce's forthcoming *Ulysses* and, when Sylvia Beach could not find a typist for Joyce's manuscript, McAlmon worked on the handwritten pages which were color-coded in red, yellow, blue, purple, and green.

> For about three pages I was painstaking and actually retyped one page to get the insertions in the right place. After that I thought,

"Molly might just as well think this or that a page or two later, or not at all," and made the insertions wherever I happened to be typing. Years later I asked Joyce if he had noticed that I'd altered the mystic arrangement of Molly's thought, and he said that he had, but agreed with my viewpoint. Molly's thoughts were irregular in several ways at best. (Quoted in Noel Riley Fitch, *Sylvia Beach and the Lost Generation*)

As Joyce became more famous, he and McAlmon drifted apart. The final blow was the curt dismissal of McAlmon and *Being Geniuses Together*. The comment had a dual sting: it relegated McAlmon to hanger-on status while it dismissed him as a writer.

Being Geniuses Together, written in 1934, was published in England in 1938 and was rescued from oblivion by Kay Boyle, who in 1968 trimmed McAlmon's original book and added her own alternating chapters which dealt with the same era and, very often, the same people and events. The final result is a marvelous account of 1920s Paris. McAlmon's view is mostly that of a wealthy, successful writer and publisher who knew everyone; Boyle's story is that of a shy, unknown writer trying to make her way.

In a prefatory note to *Being Geniuses Together*, Boyle says of McAlmon, "In the complex role of prolific writer, generous publisher, ruthless critic, exuberant drinker and dancer, outspoken enemy of the sham, sceptical friend of Joyce, Pound, Katherine Anne Porter, and countless other writers, there was never anyone quite like McAlmon around."

While McAlmon may have been a friend, skeptical or otherwise, to some, he was an outright enemy to others. One long-lasting and bitter enemy was F. Scott Fitzgerald. In *Adrift Among Geniuses*, Sanford Smoller says, "Usually sensitive, tolerant and sympathetic to others' foibles and weaknesses, Fitzgerald seemed to step out of character where McAlmon was concerned. For he virulently abused him and his work seemingly far in excess of any just retribution for a palpable offense." The offense was a major one. Fitzgerald blamed McAlmon for planting the seed in Zelda's mind that Fitzgerald was a homosexual. Indeed, Fitzgerald seemingly had an incessant, irrational fear of being a homosexual and sought advice and comfort from Hemingway and Canadian writer Morley Callaghan. This attack on his masculinity and Zelda's interest in McAlmon were enough to make Fitzgerald an enemy with clout. And this clout would manifest itself most noticeably in New York when McAlmon was seeking an American publisher for his novel *Family Panorama*.

In 1929 McAlmon set sail for America to seek an American publisher. He met with Maxwell Perkins of Scribner's. McAlmon was unaware of the forces that were at work against him. Fitzgerald, who was also being published by Scribner's, did not want McAlmon in the same stable and wrote to Perkins:

By the way McAlmon is a bitter rat and I'm not surprised at anything he does or says. He's failed as a writer and tries to fortify himself by tying up to the big boys like Joyce and Stein and despising everyone else. Part of his quarrel with Ernest [Hemingway] some years ago was because he assured Ernest that I was a fairy—God knows he shows more creative imagination in his malice than in his work. Next he told [Morley] Callaghan that Ernest was a fairy. He's a pretty good person to avoid.

and:

I took the responsibility of telling him [Hemingway] that McAlmon was at his old dirty work around New York. McAlmon, by the way, didn't have anything to do with founding *Transition*. He published Ernest's first book over here and some books of his own and did found some little magazine of no importance.

and:

God will forgive everybody—even Robert McAlmon. . . . (from *The Letters of F. Scott Fitzgerald*)

Fitzgerald's efforts paid off. Perkins passed on McAlmon's *Family Panorama*, and the book remained unpublished. McAlmon persisted in hoping that the novel would eventually be published, and even talked about its being updated to the 1940s.

Ironically, Hemingway, one of McAlmon's supposed targets according to Fitzgerald, had set up the appointment between McAlmon and Perkins. It was McAlmon's misfortune to be unaware of Hemingway's recommendation. At a dinner party, McAlmon told Perkins the story of Hemingway's admission of latent homosexuality during the 1923 trip to Spain, no doubt sealing his own fate in the process.

Through the early 1930s, McAlmon remained hopeful of a publishing breakthrough. By this time, the money from his divorce settlement had run out, and he continued to live in Europe because it was cheap. He realized he needed an American base on which to rebuild his literary reputation. He finally got *Being Geniuses Together* published in England in 1938, but no American publisher came forward. That book sank in a sea of uninterest. The Great Depression and impending war had the public's attention; few readers cared about the remembrances of a rich playboy who drank away his fortune.

McAlmon continued to knock around Europe until the outbreak of war. He made no effort to leave France, and by the time of the German occupation of Paris in June 1940, he was in ill health because of food shortages and his years of heavy drinking. Through the influence of his family and American politicians, McAlmon was released from internment and permitted to leave France. He went to Lisbon, and from there, along with other trapped Americans, finally flew back to the United States (*Adrift Among Geniuses*). Most of his books and papers, among them the manuscript of *Family Panorama*, were lost.

Back in America, McAlmon had no choice but to work for the family medical supply company. This job brought him to the Southwest for good. He worked in El Paso and Phoenix, but his deteriorating health eventually necessitated a retirement to Desert

Hot Springs, California, where he idled away his final years away from friends and the literary circles he loved. He died of pneumonia on 2 February 1956, just short of his sixtieth birthday.

Village is a novel that is composed of short stories and vignettes. It is similar in style to Sherwood Anderson's influential *Winesburg, Ohio,* although it lacks a central character. The characters in *Village* come and go and are never essential to the overall feeling evoked by the progress through fifteen years. The feelings of isolation, loneliness, stagnation, and failure run as common threads throughout many of the lives. Several of the characters come as failures to the town of Wentworth, North Dakota; other characters leave the village to find success and happiness in Chicago, Minneapolis, New York, and even Europe. School and marriage tend to be the ways out of the village for many of the young people. One boy even goes to West Point. More often, however, the young people attend the local Normal School. Those who do not venture from the village marry other local people. But the caste system, so strict in one generation, breaks down in the next through necessity. A banker's daughter marries a barber; a lawyer's son marries a farmer's daughter.

All of *Village,* however, is not bleak and desolate. McAlmon includes several highly amusing episodes. There is a long story about two boys and Daisy the cow, who has a decidedly ornery disposition. Daisy stands firm when the boys try to move her. Daisy gallops madly when the boys try to slow their pace and catch their breaths. Indeed, Gertrude Stein forwarded a letter one farmer wrote to her about Daisy: "she is the most cowy cow in literature. . . . It seems to me that she really marks the entry of cows into literature."

Another comic episode concerns a small boy who insists upon seeing a traveling road show production of *Dr. Jekyll and Mr. Hyde.* McAlmon beautifully captures the essence of boyish bravado and small-town wonder: "The night seemed peopled with fearful possibilities; human devils, and unthinkable forms that might get him. There weren't only Mr. Hydes; there were ghosts, and ghouls, and wildcats, and boogie men, who would kidnap him." After racing home through dark streets, darting from lamppost to lamppost, little Lloyd waits on his front porch for nearly ten seconds, "he dared not wait longer," and bursts into his house. His mother meets him with, "I suppose you've come in as frightened about that silly play as Elsie was. . . ." Lloyd replies, "Ah I wasn't scared." But as the mother sends Lloyd up to his room he hesitates. She asks him if he is afraid. "No mamma, but—it was cold last night in my bed, mamma. Won't you give me another cover?. . . . Come on then sonny. I see through you all right." The story is amusing and depicts the small-town attitude toward plays, actors, and all such "nonsense."

The children of Wentworth are not the only foolish beings. Many of the adult characters show little resistance to human desires and little common sense. Miss Snow, who teaches at a local school, encourages a local high school boy to make love to her. One night, he tries to break into her bedroom. She shoots at him. Another woman, vying to be the town's librarian, makes the mistake of taking rooms with Florine Watkins. Mrs. Watkins services local farmhands. The librarian loses her job. A German lady, Mrs. Simpson, won't sell her eyesore of a shack, which stands next to the Masonic Temple, because she is too lazy to move. She persists in holding out even though she is offered three times the shack's value. Local farmer Mr. Daly, owner of Daisy the cow, insists upon having a purebred dairy herd even though he cannot possibly make his money back on the cows. He goes bankrupt. Deacon Pothatch knows the value of a good crop and dutifully stores away apples, potatoes, squash, and pumpkins. These goods eventually become the target of gangs of Halloween marauders and wild teenagers. The same "boys" haul the Deacon's hay wagon down into the local creek. Pothatch allows the wagon to remain in the water all through the fall. This surprises most of the town folk. The stream eventually freezes over and becomes the local skating rink. Only then does the Deacon see fit to cut the wagon from the ice and ruin the season's skating.

Perhaps the best story in *Village* concerns the relationships in the Campbell family, which also appears to be partially auto-biographical. A tyrannical father, a sympathetic mother, and a raging son combine to create an unhappy triangle. The father reviles the son, John, for frequenting the local pool hall. The boy snaps back, "Yes I've been playing pool. What sin is there in that? What the devil do you think? You bring us to a one horse town like this to live and expect me to sit around and twiddle my fingers."

This final confrontation serves as a catalyst; the boy decides to leave home. The mother, Bessie, intercedes and asks the boy to stay until Thanksgiving. The boy reluctantly agrees and an uneasy peace exists, although the boy's mind is not changed by the appearance of tranquility. On Thanksgiving morning, John goes off to hunt with a gun. He carries the weapon toward the surrounding fields and woods. Alone in the woods, with the morning sun on his face, the boy indulges in an interior monologue:

> But what was he to do? He'd hate farm work; he'd hate office work in the city and despise the people working around him for their clerkish acquiescence. What was life all about?

And then, tiring from the exhaustive act of self-examination.

> he recalled his dream last night, in which he had been walking in a meadow filled with the live bodies of people he could scarcely avoid trampling on. They had all evaporated as he tried to touch them with his hand.

John is apart from his world; he cannot be a member of his own family or of the human race.

> Where were there people who could mean much to him? He'd observed enough lives not to believe anybody got much out of living.

And then, after a momentary exhilaration during which the sun warms him and the morning breezes stir his awareness of life:

He felt his youngness, his vitality of resistance that was, and for this time would be, insistently proud and reckless of all thought. People! None of them could matter to him. He didn't need, like his father, to be disturbed about worshipping a god to have an after life. Somewhere else, another time, amongst other people, he would be—

This story is revealing. It may stem from the boyish yearnings of McAlmon's youth on the prairies, but it also mirrors the adult McAlmon's attitudes toward the world. One of the consistent views one gets from reading the memoirs and biographies about the Paris years is that McAlmon was cold, calculating, and aloof. This image persists despite his facade of being a drinking buddy and jovial host. McAlmon was, as most people are, a complicated personality; the public demeanor and outer shell hid an un-self-confident man with a bitter soul.

Other elements in the story point to its being autobiographical. The mother's name, Bessie, is McAlmon's mother's name. And there are more similarities. She is a sympathetic character, a victim of her marriage and of the times. As the story branches out, the reader learns of Bessie's happy life before she married. Her marriage to a lawyer produces many children, but life for Bessie remains unhappy because of the violent temper of her husband.

Although the professions of the two fathers are different, the core of the differences between father and son is the same—religion. McAlmon and his counterpart, John, rebel against the strict religious upbringing and against the society that produces such repressed lives.

During a visit to Taos, New Mexico, in 1927, McAlmon met Mabel Dodge and wrote glowingly of the physical beauty of New Mexico, its Indians, and pueblos. Yet McAlmon could see past the facades of pueblos and sunsets and mountain vistas; he could see the hypocrisy of America. McAlmon saw politicians who cheated Indians, sheriffs who drank bootleg whiskey and then arrested the bootleggers, and the old, fundamental duplicity of puritan morality. Ultimately McAlmon concluded that Mable Dodge and the others of her art colony simply contaminated the natural primitive beauty of New Mexico with "arty" civilized savagery (*Adrift Among Geniuses*).

What the world saw in Robert McAlmon was a man who was a supreme cynic, a caustic, sometimes bitter, hard-drinking writer who had failed at his craft. But underneath that cold exterior, McAlmon was a man who saw his world with a clear eye. If he sounds to us now jaded, uncaring, and belligerent, it must be remembered that McAlmon considered himself to be a man who was always honest. When his honesty was leveled at others, it was often viewed as being spite or maliciousness, and McAlmon often put himself in this same harsh spotlight of truth. One night, when McAlmon was carousing with Morley Callaghan, and after the usual overindulgence in drinks, McAlmon blurted out, "I'm bisexual myself, like Michelangelo, and I don't give a damn who knows it."

Of course McAlmon did care, but his personality prevented him from playing the societal games that most of us accept as politeness. McAlmon never wrote about his own sexuality nor did he write about his marriage to Bryher. There were some private areas in his life. In his fiction, on the other hand, McAlmon did write about all facets of life, and he did not back off from examining deviant behavior of all kinds. McAlmon's own character comes through in many of his fictive personalities, male and female, and in this respect the aware reader can cull the bits and pieces of McAlmon's life from his novels and short stories.

In the Thanksgiving story in *Village* McAlmon's youthful thoughts can be seen in John Campbell's monologue. Toward the end of the novel, the reader is told that Peter Reynalds, "if remembered or mentioned at all by any of the old time younger people, was thought to be leading a dissolute life, somewhere in Europe, probably Paris, which was known to be a horribly immoral city. He had always been fast anyway, a great drinker, and forever on the verge of being involved in some scandal. . . ."

A Note on the Editing

Although McAlmon's books were plagued by poor typesetting and careless proofreading, which resulted in books with far too many typographical errors, the editing of this reprint has been kept to a minimum in order to maintain, as much as possible, the original flavor of McAlmon's writing. Obvious misspellings and typos have been corrected; some punctuation has been standardized; and only in a few places have I eliminated superfluous punctuation in order to make a passage read more clearly.

Edward N. S. Lorusso
Albuquerque
July 1989

Works Cited

Fitch, Noel Riley. *Sylvia Beach and the Lost Generation.* New York: W. W. Norton & Co., 1985.

Fitzgerald, F. Scott. *The Letters of F. Scott Fitzgerald.* Edited by Andrew Turnbull. New York: Dell Publishing Co., 1966.

Ford, Hugh. *Published in Paris.* New York: Macmillan Publishing Co., 1975.

Kenner, Hugh. *The Pound Era.* Berkeley and Los Angeles: University of California Press, 1971.

McAlmon, Robert. *Being Geniuses Together* With Kay Boyle. San Francisco: North Point Press, 1984.

McAlmon, Robert. *Post-Adolescence.* Paris: Contact Publishing Co., 1923.

McAlmon, Robert. *Village.* Paris: Contact Publishing Co., 1924.

Smoller, Sanford. *Adrift Among Geniuses.* University Park: Pennsylvania State University Press, 1975.

The Books of Robert McAlmon

Explorations. London: The Egoist Press, 1921.

A Hasty Bunch. Paris: Contact Publishing Co., 1922.

A Companion Volume. Paris: Contact Publishing Co., 1923.

Post-Adolescence. Paris: Contact Publishing Co., 1923.

Village. Paris: Contact Publishing Co., 1924.

Distinguished Air. Paris: Contact Editions at the Three Mountain Press, 1925.

The Portrait of a Generation. Paris: Contact Editions, Three Mountain Press, 1926,

North America, Continent of Conjecture. Paris: Contact Editions, 1929.

The Indefinite Huntress and Other Stories. Paris: Crosby Continental Editions, The Black Sun Press, 1932.

Not Alone Lost. Norfolk, Conn.: New Directions, 1937.

Being Geniuses Together. London: Secker and Warburg, 1938.

McAlmon and the Lost Generation: A Self Portrait, edited and with commentary by Robert E. Knoll. Lincoln: University of Nebraska Press, 1962.

There Was a Rustle of Black Silk Stockings. [Reprint of *Distinguished Air*]. New York: Belmont Books, 1963.

THE BOOKS OF ROBERT MCALMON

Being Geniuses Together: 1920–1930, revised and with supplementary chapters by Kay Boyle. Garden City· Doubleday & Co., 1968.

Books Published by Contact Publishing
Robert McAlmon, Publisher

1922
A *Hasty Bunch* by Robert McAlmon

1923
A *Companion Volume* by Robert McAlmon
Post-Adolescence by Robert McAlmon
Two Selves by Bryher
Lunar Baedecker by Mina Loy
Three Stories and Ten Poems by Ernest Hemingway
Twenty-five Poems by Marsden Hartley
Spring and All by William Carlos Williams

1924
Village by Robert McAlmon

1925
Contact Collection of Contemporary Writers
Ashe of Rings by Mary Butts
My First Thirty Years by Gertrude Beasley

A *Hurried Man* by Emanuel Carnevali
The Making of Americans by Gertrude Stein

1926
Palimpsest by H. D. (Hilda Doolittle)
The Portrait of a Generation by Robert McAlmon
The Eater of Darkness by Robert M. Coates
Ladies Almanack by Djuna Barnes

1929
North America, Continent of Conjecture by Robert McAlmon
Sailors Don't Care by Edwin M. Lanham
Quaint Tales of the Samurai by Saikaku Ibara (tr. Ken Sato)

1931
The Dream Life of Balso Snell by Nathanael West

VILLAGE

Book One

Beyond the outskirts of the Village, Wentworth, the wind blew, if not more boisterously than in the city proper, with a sweep uninterrupted by dwelling houses, or other obstacles. Already the gloss and dazzle of snow, which had fallen but two days ago, was dulled by the dust, which whirlpools and hurricanes of rash rushing winds had swept across the land for over a day and a half, after a three foot fall of snow. In the afternoon a lull occurred; now again, at ten o'clock in the evening, the gale was up, tearing into the snow and throwing it into banks that fill the air in spares of ground upon which uncovered grey-white snow lay scantily.

Weird snow music, snow wind clamour, shrill shriek of cold whiteness shattered by a highmoaning vermillion calliope wail. Where are the gray wolf packs? The herd of bison that thundered in catapulting panic across the plains?

Fifty miles away lay the Indian reservation, with its degenerating remnants of a once wild and arrogant race. No evidence of will or desire remains for the eye to observe. Apathy and dull carelessness, without the consciousness of indifference, are all that can be discerned.

Few farmers can be coming into the village for the next few days.

Not till the snow has packed down so that horses can plow their way through the covered roads; not till need or the daring of more audacious souls has caused a few farmers to remake the roadways, will many leave their farm homeside fires to come and market in Wentworth. Salt pork and potatoes, salt pork and sauerkraut, milk and soggy bread, will suffice as a diet for German, Polish, Swedish, and unexpectant farm families in these cold days surely, when they have sufficed as their main food always.

To be sure, though, there is little doubt that Ike Sorenson will attempt to drive his faithful team to town from his ranch eight miles out. It's not to be thought that either wind, or snow, or cold, or rain, or heat, or hurricane, or blizzard, will keep old Ike from crusading forth for his weekly drunk-on. He will have his hard liquor though the world be crashing to its end.

"Come on Ouija, tell me. Am I going to West Point, or Annapolis, or not to either?" Gene Collins pleaded, admonishing Peter Reynalds to be sure that he wasn't pushing the signal table with his hand.

"Honest Injun Gene," Peter swore, "didn't we promise to play fair? I'd like to know as well as you what makes this thing move, and I sure don't push it, unless just kind of knowing the answer we want, something in us makes us do it when we think we aren't."

Peter's too flower-like face was intense as he watched for the Ouija board to answer Gene's question. His baby clear blue eyes glowed in the dim light of the the room, but even in interest his mind was dispersed, as some removed portion of it strained to dramatize this incident into romance.

"I can't understand it," Gene said. "Do you suppose there is electricity in us, and that what we want answered gets back and forth between us—because I haven't known what answer you wanted to lots of your questions."

"O well, I guess you and I know the kind of thing both of us want pretty well. That's why I like you so much better than Alison

4

Parker, or Stan Jones. They haven't any curiosity about nothing. God, I'll be glad when I'm through high school and can go away to the city—maybe—but if I go to college I'll have to earn my money because the folks can't help me. Three more years. Maybe I can save up some before then. Let's you and I start taking in the harvest fields next year—or get a job somewhere together next summer."

"But we'd miss the Chautauqua season, and that's the most fun there ever is around this damned old burg," Gene answered.

"Yes, but we might get jobs there—in the hotel, or at the popstand, or something."

Mrs. Collins, Gene's mother, came into the room to say good-night. She was retiring early, exhausted, as she might well be, carrying her great flabby person about all day. Though her loose form did not reveal it, she also expected another baby in two months' time, a surprise to her at so late a year in her life as her youngest child Renée was already eight years old. Before retiring however she wanted to give Peter Reynalds a little talk on family, since he seemed to be most about with Gene now of any boy in town, and she wanted him to appreciate who it was he was associating with.

"I'm not one to brag," she said, "or to want my children to be snobs, but I just tell them about their forebears so they will know they can hold their heads up anywhere they go. Of course the debt will never be paid, but if the French government it or we would pay back all it owes to our family from away back since the Revolution, we'd be one of the wealthiest families in the world. I don't remember very clearly, but some ancestor of ours lent some king or other all kinds of money years and years back. We aren't one of those families which can't trace back more than a generation; though I'm very democratic myself, and not one to boast."

Fifteen-year-old Gene looked sheepish, and mumbled: "Peter doesn't give a darn about all that rot, mother," but Mrs. Collins pattered on for a few minutes. Her mind and her conversation never stayed fixed on any one point for long, so that before finally saying goodnight, she was rambling on about the marriage that her father, the gay, rakish old Mr. Dubois, had made. "He wrote me the woman was wealthy but I've heard nothing from him since, and from other reports that are drifting back I'm thinking both he and that Atlantic City widow played a joke on each other, each pretending to have money they don't have."

This point however didn't interest her long either. She retired, unable to find an interested audience, and tolerant with fat good-nature of her son's irritated indifference to her efforts at being friendly to his companion.

Eight-year-old Renée Collins came into the room, not knowing what to do with herself, and still not ready to go to bed.

Renée wasn't wanted around by the boys, but they were amiable and told her she could stay to watch if she'd sit quietly. This however was not little Renée's style.

"I know something about Loraine, I know something about Loraine, but I'm not going to tell you," she said in enthusiastic secrecy. When not coaxed to reveal her secret she however went on with it after a pause, "she's sitting out on the closed-in porch with her beau, and she's sitting on his lap, and he kissed her. I heard him."

"Ah, keep still," Gene told his sister mildly. "What do you want to snoop around for?" He was afraid that Peter might be shocked at this tale on his older sister, and it wouldn't be nice for his best friend to think his sister *that* kind of a girl, though of course Peter knew that most any girl started to fuss and cuddle by the time she was Loraine's age. He knew too that Loraine had been going with Elmer Jones for three years which probably meant that the two would marry each other.

Renée finally departed for bed; and Peter said he'd have to be going home or risk getting the devil from his mother for staying out so late.

"I wonder if the things the Ouija Board told us will come true," Gene asked. "I almost wish they don't because Ouija says I go to Annapolis, and that you don't, and we ought to be friends all our life."

"Yes," Peter brooded, sentimentally sad about their friendship. "But we won't even be together so much this year after Christmas, because you'll make the basketball team sure and be around with all the fellows who are athletic."

"Why don't you try for it too, Peter? You could make the second team, or the third anyway maybe," Gene encouraged.

Peter felt a bitterness swell up in him. "What do you think . . . I'm not going to be a hanger-on. If I'd lived in this damn town before, or anywhere else where fellows play football and baseball I probably wouldn't have wanted to get into the games. I don't see that a guy has to do that to amount to anything." A moment of antagonism towards Gene existed in him as he thought that Gene was apt to be boastful about his athletic prowess, and his talking about how he'd sure make the football team next year. The antagonism died however as he came to the door of the house in preparation to depart. Then a regret at having to go home changed his mood.

"I don't suppose our family will stay long in this town anyway; we never stay long anywhere; dad's always moving us about. I'll be glad when I'm old enough to go away and make my own living. My older brother tells me he'll help me get started, and he's in Detroit now. Sometimes I feel like running away and going there, but he'd send me back because of mother, though he had a hell of a scrap with dad when he was my age, and went away for good himself."

"But what about Carrie?" Gene said, joking a little. "You couldn't leave her."

"Ah rats, I'm not so stuck on her as all that. I'm not nearly so mushy as you are about Marie, but she makes me laugh. Gosh, but she's bossy though, but I like that. Marie's too sweet for me. That's what you like though I guess."

"It's just having a girl, that's all it is with me, and Marie is pretty. . . . I wish you'd stay a little while longer, up in my den. There's a fire up there. You can tell your mother you waited for the storm to calm down. I feel like talking lots tonight."

The boys went up to Gene's den. It was quieter there, on the side of the house away from the gale. The wood whispered as it burned in the fireplace, and now and then some damp or knotted portion of it whined as the hot fire reached it. The two rested themselves upon cushions before it, and were silent for a time, as they gazed into the fire.

"What is a guy to think, and plan for later on?" Peter broke the silence at last, speaking softly. "The city! I passed through Chicago once when I was seven, and it bewildered me, but I remember the impression, and always want to get away to some city now; but my brother doesn't think much of it; neither do my two older sisters. I don't know what I want to be when I grow up. I'd kind of like to be only a hobo—a highclass one, and travel all over the world. Wouldn't it be nice if you and I broke loose and got on board a ship and travelled around for several years together?"

"I would too—after next year—if I make the football team—though of course then I'd like to make good at that."

"It'll always be like that, something to hold you."

"I'd go around travelling with you, because you're game; but I wouldn't with most of the fellows in this one-horse town. You and I get on best with each other of anybody I've ever known. Maybe it's just that we're getting older."

"Funny you know. We knew each other for two years before we hardly ever noticed each other. I always liked your looks though" Peter said. "The first day I saw you, when you came into our class room, the seventh grade, I thought you were awfully funny looking. Your neck is so short, you know. But when I got used to that I liked your looks. I guess it was because Lloyd Scott and I were so thick at that time, and he didn't like you—was jealous because you played baseball better than he—that we didn't get chummy till we got in high school."

"Oh, we were just kids—and I never stuck around much except during school hours," Gene answered, and hesitated for a moment, reflecting upon something he wanted to ask, then he continued speaking: "you'll think I'm wanting to be funny, or that I'm being nasty or something, but I wonder—you know—well you know what happens to fellows our age—I wonder if it's happened to you yet."

Peter answered quickly: "I guess so; I thought Chemo had talked to you. I told him about the scare I had one night after I got to bed, and I thought something had burst in me. He said he'd been afraid when that happened to him, and went to see Dr. Douglas who only laughed and said: "That's all right Chemo, my boy. You just take a girl and you'll be all right," and Chemo thought he had to or he'd be sick. But you don't have to at all because your dreams take care of you."

"I'm glad I asked you," Gene said. "I've wanted to talk to somebody who wouldn't get funny about it. You know lots more than I do because I guess you've got older brothers."

"Rats, they don't tell me anything. I read books on what boys should know, and look up words in our medical dictionary."

The conversation drifted to talk about colleges they would go to—with many names and much indecision. They seemed very near and very far from each other. Peter wondered to himself if he really liked Gene as a friend as he liked Lloyd Scott, to whom he'd acted indifferently lately, simply because Lloyd was continuing on at the Normal School, while he was at the Central High School, and the two schools were rivals. The unspoken understanding that had existed between him and Loyd was not here with Gene. He almost resented his affection for Gene, he wondered if he'd have liked him at all if many other boys of his own age were about. It was simply that all of the other boys in their classes at high school were such dumbheads. Gene had an attraction for him however that Lloyd had never had. He wondered, was that simply now, and because both of them were adolescent? But if that was so, why did it exist more between him and Gene than between him and other boys in that period? He saw that Gene felt about him as he did about Gene; attracted, and antagonistic too. That was rivalry, and jealousy, because the two of them led their class easily.

It was one o'clock before Peter noticed the time, and in a panic jumped up saying he had to rush home. Gene wished him to stay all night. They could phone his mother.

"No, no, not now. It's too late," Peter said. "Mother will be in bed but listening for me to come in. She'd give me hell tomorrow if I'd phone now, and I couldn't say why I didn't phone earlier."

Still with a mood of introspection in him Peter put on his coat and was out into the night. The door of Gene's house had closed on him, and the light of the house was lost in the darkness of night before Peter was actively aware of the terrifying coldness of this North Dakota night. He grit his teeth against the wind, breathing heavily, trying to keep his mouth closed and to breathe through his nostrils, as it seemed that his breath would become an icicle in his mouth if he puffed against the wind. A gale blew about him. Sleet which had begun to fall some time before, unnoticed by him in his intimate talk with Gene, swirled about and into him, cutting the tender flesh of his cheeks. Tears froze along his eyelashes and in the corner of his eyes. He realized by the time he had struggled a block that he was in the midst of a North Dakota blizzard. Holding his hand out in front of him to see if he could see it—as he'd heard that one cannot in a blizzard—he was unable to, because of the darkness, the black coldness of the wind, and the swirl of snow. A despair began to settle into his heart; ink filled his lungs. He could never reach home—five blocks. He was lost. He did not know which direction he was going.

However he struggled on, thinking of lying down in the snow and letting it cover him, but realizing that this was just a self-pitying thought too, and that he never would give up unless he were frozen. At one moment he found that he'd gone in a circle but realized in coming against a building that it was one of the old Normal School buildings. That located him for himself so that he knew in what direction to go. Soon he was at home, and the storm was sufficient so that his mother accepted it as explanation for his staying away so long.

"But you will have to stop going to that Collins boy's house at night," she told him. "You always stay too late there whatever the weather. I don't know but what you are playing pool, or gambling. It's absurd for boys of your age to be staying up till one and two o'clock in the morning, and how do I know you are at the Collins'? I don't know the family."

"Why don't you call up their house and find out when you don't know?" Peter said, hard within himself. There was no use, he believed, in trying to explain to his mother how essential it was for him and Gene to talk, and talk, just to find out what the other was thinking, and that there should be something to think about, other than just the routine of going through days of existence.

Wentworth lay in the midst of North Dakota prairies, and at the beginning of the epoch written of was recuperating from a period of famine years, through which innumerable families were forced to desert their claims, farms, and homes, even in villages. People who, failures in the East, had come here in the past to a pioneer life, struggled through one or two winters with little food to eat, and, reduced to cowchips for fuel, were generally forced to give up the struggle or have the starvation which confronted them relentlessly close in upon them.

Now again, ten years after these years of food shortage, crop failure, stock loss, and climatic hardship, the country about was beginning to become a prosperous one; and settlers had for the last six or seven years begun coming once more to homesteads, of which the acres surrounding yielded profitable crops,—corn, wheat, oats, barley, and produce,—potatoes and onions mainly.

Within the boundaries of Wentworth lived some five thousand inhabitants; the Fords and the Higgins, pauperish families of innumerable offspring; the Crawshaws, a poor lot also, but with some money-earning members amongst its large brood; the La Brecs, the father of which lot was a hardworking mason, with a negligent wife, and impishly dirty children. All of these families were the slum populace of the village, without enough character amongst the men members for them to be even town toughs, and with girl members whose destinies would seem to be that of being wait-resses, prostitutes, or the slovenly wives and mothers of families no disreputable as their families of this present generation. Time alone however could judge that. Already Lila La Brec, a girl with brickish-hued hair, a pallorous, freckled face, a thin but graceful body, and a jaunty air, had surprised the town by turning from a vulgar-mouthed and homely little girl into an attractive young lady, neatly dressed, and capable of attracting travelling salesmen away from such girls as Alberta Kingston, and Lottie Schmidt, both of whom, while probably fast, and undoubtedly indiscreet, were the daughters of men of wealth and standing in the community. It was the custom of many girls in town to meet the incoming trains at the depot to see what stop-over passengers were arriving this time; and most girls who met the trains were ready to be picked up by adventuresome travelling salesmen who attracted them, if the salesmen were discreet about their approaches.

North of the railroad track, and the depot, most of Wentworth lay, though the coalyards, grain elevators, the mill, and a few families were situated in the block or so before the town limits that stretched from the south side. To the east, south side, lived the loafing Ford and Higgins families in each of which were not less than fifteen existing in a two room shack. If all of either family ever congregated in full force, which never happened, there'd have been twenty five people in that particular shack, as relatives, bastard children, and an extraordinarily large family in either case made up the quantity. However the grown-up girls managed at various times to have jobs as waitresses at railroad stations in nearby towns, or at little hotels; a hardpressed wife now and then had been known to try one of them as a house servant; but they didn't last long on any job, not even at whoring, which both Flossie Ford and Gertie Higgins had tried. Their temperaments simply were not given to persistence.

To encompass and sociologize Wentworth, it is best to start from the boundary lines and close in upon its heart, if villages have hearts. Farms at intervals of one, two, three, five, seven and many miles lay around the extensive prairie lands surrounding the village, the county seat of Sand County. The distance separating the farms depended upon the distance from Wentworth which might be under comment.

The outskirts of the village to the north was a respectable, even a highclass neighborhood, since it was on that boundary line that the eminent Branch family in years past had elected to build their ten room red brick mansion, which for years stood as a symbol of grandeur in town. They by this time had however departed, taking with them all their possessions but the red brick house, and their legend of New England culture and respectability.

The east and west edges of town were also respectably the locations upon which dwelt a dairy farmer, and numerous elderly, law abiding, retired farmers, whose children might at moments break loose into wild escapades, or might through a course in village metropolis influence degenerate into poolhall loungers, or—if they were girls—become young ladies seen on the main streets too often; but these were possibilities which confronted all parents of Wentworth.

The La Brecs, living near the center of town, were recognizable as La Brecs always, as all of them were freckled with some manner of sandy, brick, or carrot coloured hair that passed as red, and all of them had the La Brec leanness and sharpness of facial feature, which in some instances approached beauty, had it not been a La Brec possessing that beauty. The Crawshaws, down a block from them, were also usually recognizable as Crawshaws because of family type, a tawnier, more indolent, less impertinently slovenly type than the La Brec species. The children in this family were older, too; and two of them had "made good" in a manner, since Tom Crawshaw, who started at fifteen as a brakeman, had managed to become a railroad engineer at a salary of one hundred and fifty dollars a month, and this added to his social position greatly. He was also good to look at; no one would have been particularly shocked if a girl of good family had started to go around with him, since marriageable men were scarce. He however apparently liked some girl out of town.

Paula Crawshaw too, the oldest girl in the family, had made herself acceptable in town, if she wished to stay there. After finishing high school she went to the city, and when she returned two years later, for a visit, she was as well dressed a girl as there was in town, and it was soon known that she had a good position in Minneapolis as secretary to an attorney. Girls who had only nodded to her as she was growing up with them in high school were disposed to be friendly, as they were curious about her experiences in Minneapolis, to which city many of them were deciding they'd better go if they didn't want to petrify in Wentworth as old maids.

Up and down Egan Avenue, the main street, every young person with a feeling for social life would stroll on a decent day, winter or summer. Along this avenue, on the upper portion, were the four grocery stores of the town; the department, dry-goods and grocery store, drug store, the poolhall, where all young men congregated winter afternoons especially, and nights all through the year; the doctors' and attorneys' building; and across the corner from the poolhall, the postoffice, where at five in the afternoon anybody was apt to appear, ostensibly to get mail.

Cutting the middle of the four city blocks of Egan Avenue was Fourth Street, and upon it the Grand Theatre, in which what few theatrical entertainments came to town appeared. Here too it was that Mr. Goyer held his loom-end sales for three years, until housewives began to grumble that for all his advertised bargains his wares were expensive; and here it was that Gorgona, the hypnotist, magician, and psychic lecturer, appeared every six months or so, until the belief that he was a complete fake, and a bum show, caused people to stop going to his performances. Here too various plays appeared; musical comedies with sure fire song hits such as

what's the use of dreaming
dreams of rosy hue
what's the use of dreaming
dreams that never will come true
you may have your millions,
etc.

Classic drama was presented once in a while here, but Shakespeare was not successful in Wentworth, even when Touchstone threw ten apples away after snatching them from Audrey's hand for low comedy. The townspeople liked better dramas of purity and seduction, or dramas about women with pasts.

The Woman of Mystery was a play that always drew, though it had showed yearly at the Grand for the last ten years. It was the story of a country girl who, wronged by an older man, left her village home and became famous in the great places of the world. In the last act it is revealed that she, a magnificently dressed lady, who fascinates all men, is the mother, and not the aunt of the young man in the play; it is further revealed that the rich and famous man who is in her coils, is her seducer and the father of her son. She at the last moment, torn by doubts, rather than take her rightful revenge upon him, relents and forgives, discovering at that moment that love she once had for him, which he so abused, still can flame.

Another play of the wild West was liked by the younger generation of Wentworth. In the third act of this play, Kate Andrews, a cowman's daughter, saves her fiancé, David Holcom, from the ruffians, who have bound him hand and foot to a tree which grows, scantily rooted, above a canyon chasm. Gradually the tree's roots are tearing loose from the soil because of a pendulum hammer slowly beating against the trunk of the tree. Just as the tree is about to rip from its roots and dash David to the bottom of the chasm, Kate appears across the way. With her shotgun, and six well-placed shots, she rends the rope binding David, and he with a mighty leap catches a grape vine and swings across the chasm to Kate and safety. This play never failed to bring excited warnings to the hero and heroine from some member of the audience.

Outside the entrance to the theatre, on the second story, hung an exterior balcony. Until a boy was fifteen it was deemed discreditable of him to ever pay for his entrance to a performance. He should instead, not to be a fraidcat and a sissy, climb to the balcony, and enter the gallery of the theatre through the window. This action on the part of a boy over fifteen however lacked dignity, as did indeed going to a play even, unless it were with a gang who went intending to hoot and shout, and raise hell in general.

It was only in the last five years that social life of any tone had begun to exist in Wentworth; but that five years! Now decidedly amongst the generation just in, or just out of high school, there was no doubt who was who, and who was tony, and who was nobody.

There were ten girls who were *it*; six others who were companions of *it*; and seven more who might on certain occasions approach *it*. It was humanly impossible that all of the ten girls who were *it*—Wentworth high society—should be beautiful, so the schedule was arranged this way: Helaine Blair was the most beautiful girl in town; Netta Fitzgerald the most graceful; Mary Warden the most dignified; Gertrude Freeman the most comic and the best fellow; and Naomi Morris the most intellectual. The other five of the ten who were *it*, were younger sisters of this five, and did not need to be rated for the next year or so. Lela and Katherine Bell were companions of *it* simply on the strength of their evident intelligence, and the fact that their mother kept an exclusive boarding house at which was apt to stay any eligible young professional or business man who newly located in town, and this, giving Lela and Katherine first chance to operate their wiles, made them not to be neglected as friends. The Johnston girls were companions of *it* mainly on looks, though their father was well off too; but he was Protestant, and the *it* girls all belonged to Catholic families, for a three year period, until the lookers seemed to be coming mainly from Protestant families. As the young swains of town followed where looks lead, the Catholic *its* had to forget sectarian principle a bit and open up their ranks. But that is a history of slow and subtle evolution.

Helaine Blair was *it* on beauty solely; her widowed mother had nothing; her sister, older, and quite as beautiful, had to make her living as a clerk in the town department store, but Helaine had more vivacity and dazzle than her sister. It was evident she'd get her pick of men in town. Her orange hair, her orange brown eyes with a fiery coquettish gleam in them, her swanlike neck, and gazelle gesture of body, were things that wouldn't let her be passed up. She was the *it* of which all the other *its* and near *its* were envious because the thought that she had a voice of operatic quality, added to her beauty, and she was aloof.

Netta Fitzgerald's father was town hardware dealer, an owner of several farms, and a man of much wealth. Her elder sister had married a prominent attorney in Minneapolis.

Mary Warden's father was president of the County Bank, and presumably the richest man in town; she and Netta were the leading *its* who were not so aloof as Helaine Blair.

Gertrude Freeman's father was town jeweler, with not much wealth, with a dull, and nastily dissolute son, and with a bad reputation himself; but Gertrude was Catholic, comic, a good fellow with an Irish sense of humour, and apt to marry one of the Warden boys from all appearances.

Naomi Morris had parents of an old New England family; calm, cameo good looks, a quiet manner, and a brain. She was *it* on the basis of being a puzzle to the others, and on the acquired knowledge that however wild an escapade any of them had been on, she evinced no disapproval, and was good at inventing explanations to be passed on to irate parents.

However, almost as soon as a high society set established the fact to the observation of onlookers that it existed, and social lines were drawn, the ones constituting the sacred set, found themselves needing to struggle to remain The Society Group. For within a year there was evidence of rival grace, beauty, wealth, dignity, wit, and family, coming to dispute their claim; and girls who'd been children, were suddenly young ladies, and young ladies who set a pace in the matter of dress and gaiety of life that promised to relegate the reigning belles to the scrap bag. Netta Fitzgerald was away for ten months teaching school out of town; Mary Warden spent the winter in the city; Naomi Morris too taught school out of town; they returned to find that as far as social supremacy was concerned they might as well now stay out of town. A younger generation was going the pace, and looked on them as old girls who were simply marking time till somebody came along and married them—if that ever happened, and the chances were as much against it as for it, unless they consented to marry country bumpkins.

Mr. Frank Jenkins, aged thirty nine, height five foot eleven inches, weight two hundred forty pounds, took up his tennis racket and started out of the house towards the tennis court, where he was sure that at least the Rev. James Robinson would be, if Henry Scott was not there. Frank Jenkins' light chestnut hair curled in disarray upon his pulpy head; his piggy small blue eyes glistened above a putty nose.

Walking as quickly as a softly fat frame let him, Frank nearly collided into old Mrs. Granger. At first, he started to bow in easy recognition, which he immediately changed to a stiff "good evening, Mrs. Granger," as he recalled that she owed his coal firm some thirty dollars for wood and coal delivered her during the previous winter months. She, bent and harried looking, answered his greeting almost furtively, hesitating as to whether she should stop and explain that within a month she would be able to settle the account. Instead however she kept her hands nervously in place, holding each other folded across her upper abdomen as though she were chilly even in this hot weather. And she walked on, too conscious of a censorious gaze or thought following her as she retreated. Humiliated at her poverty she felt yet an impulse of resentment at Mr. Jenkins. She did not like or trust the man; it wasn't only because of his size that she felt he was bestial; she was sure it wasn't that alone. How could he so soon after his wife's suicide be setting a date for his marriage with that woman, his mistress, who had been the cause of it. And the first Mrs. Jenkins had been so charming and generous. She could overlook the fact that Mr. Jenkins was a man of passion if he was that, but she believed that he was only a man of oily sensuality, and it was unfair in life that so swinish a person could drive an honest, sweet woman like his first wife to her death. And his dealings in Wentworth through his coal company were reported not to be always decent. Certainly her bill was much higher than it would have been if she had had ready money to pay it in the beginning, or if she were a person so fixed financially that he hadn't known he could browbeat her.

The resentment towards Mr. Jenkins passed however as she walked on down the street. Other worries came into her mind. She must try and persuade the baker to take some of her cooking and display it for sale so as to have more money with which to run the household and keep the children at school. Mr. Osgood, the baker, was a kindly man, and she of course would not cook things that competed with his line.

Frank Jenkins found Henry Scott, postmaster, and chief attorney of Wentworth, playing tennis with his sixteen year old boy, Lloyd. As grave-faced, reserved Mr. Scott was rather indifferent to Frank's suggestion that they have a set later, Frank went across the street to see if the Rev. Robinson, pastor of the First Presbyterian church, would not play with him. Regardless of rumours that his tennis playing was being criticized by some of the ladies in his congregation—by Mrs. Lewis mainly—the pastor was ready for a game. Soon his tall, lithe figure was bounding about the court energetically, as Mr. Jenkins, in spite of fatness, played a hard game. Within fifteen minutes Mr. Scott and Jake Rankin joined them in a game of doubles, until they considered it too dark to see the balls, whereupon all of them went downtown to the Commercial Club to play billiards, chat, smoke, or read, leaving the court for youngsters to fool on so long as they did so in bare feet or in tennis shoes.

It was but eight o'clock, still light enough for over an hour to have played on had they actually wished. Down Egan Avenue innumerable people were strolling to have the benefit of the cool evening air. Groups of young people were seated on the green lawns along the way. The seven-forty train from the city had arrived, and young ladies whose chief pleasure it was to meet incoming trains were loitering on their way back from the depot. The curly, black-haired Alberta Kingston, as usual, had picked up a travelling salesman with whom she'd amuse herself as long as he was in town. She looked dashing, a vivid, but not a pretty picture. Erik Watson, whose father was only a bank clerk, but who'd managed to send his son to college—the first boy from Wentworth to go to college—came tottering down the street, tipsy. It was easy to see that he was doing his best to drown his sorrow because Rose Borrows had jilted him. Rose was Helaine Blair's only real rival for astounding beauty, but Rose spent most of her time out of town, having been educated at a girls' private school. The drunkenness of Erik would mean a good deal of chatter for Mrs. Lewis, who would of course see it from behind her curtains or from her front veranda, from which she surveyed and censured village goings-on during the warm summer months.

Arrived at the Commercial Club the Rev. Robinson turned back, not so much unwilling to expose himself to further criticism by mingling with the laity, as preferring to read rather than to indulge in mediocre parley with Mr. Jenkins. Mr. Jenkins and Mr. Scott went upstairs, and seated themselves to smoke a cigar while waiting for a billiard table to be free.

"I hear you're moving to Minneapolis to go into the brokerage business, Frank," Mr. Scott queried.

"The boys want to go to college, Alec now, and Allen in a year or so. I think it's best. It would be different, you understand, here, with a second Mrs. Jenkins, after the unfortunate incident—ah— er—," Frank answered, leaving any mention of his first wife's name out of the remark. Mr. Scott too wished to evade the subject. He'd thought the year before that the Jenkins marriage and family had been one of the best examples of success in wedlock about town. His wife had been quite intimate with Mrs. Jenkins, and his boy had played with Allen Jenkins. The abrupt suicide had quite shocked him.

"What are you doing with your grain and coal business? It's on the market I suppose. Some of my clients might be interested in buying it over."

"Yes, any offers from you, Henry, I'll appreciate. My partner, Mr. Colton, will handle it for a time. No hurry, of course. How trustworthy partners are we can't always say, you know Henry. If you'll keep a watchful eye," Frank conversed, assuming a lowered, confidential tone. Mr. Scott nodded, recalling that Mr. Colton, Frank's partner, had been complaining to him too that Frank's actions were none too confidence-inspiring. Scott however commented:

"Well, Frank, business is business you know, and every man likes to do as well by himself as he can. I think Colton is fairly competent, and you have a watchful eye for guarding your own interests I guess. Ha, ha, ha, I can't see you being done out of much that you think is yours rightfully. You never grab the dirty end of the stick."

Jenkins laughed uneasily. "Yes, I suppose it's good that I'm going to the city. That unfortunate incident—everybody is disposed to suspect my motives a little now. It's natural I suppose, though how I—mental sickness you know—"

Mr. Scott did not answer, but reflected that before Mrs. Jenkins' suicide he'd always thought of Frank as a man to watch closely in a business deal.

"You know I've been hearing that old Mrs. Granger has been fooling the whole town. It's said she inherited quite a fortune three or four years back, and is just miserly. She owes me a coal bill for quite a sum. I think I'd better come down on her," Frank spoke again.

"You can't trust a rumour like that; she owes quite a number of bills about town but I've never been able to locate anything but her furniture which is attachable. I suspect her poverty is real. It's only that her older children, who support themselves, are extravagant in their dress. The elder girl particularly is quite apt to be the victim of jealous criticism on the part of women who like to talk, though she's not in town often, and must keep up appearances to hold the position she does in the city. I can't say more, as an attorney, but I have private information on her family. I will say though that she doesn't get much help from the husband. You may have noticed that he isn't around with them now."

The clubroom was filled by now, nine-thirty, with business men and young men—idlers, and boys free from school for the summer. It was impossible for the two men to continue a conversation dealing with privacies concerning debts and business, so the conversation shifted.

"They say young Tom Warden was pretty hot about the chivaree party the kids in town put up on him the night he married Edith Burton. It seems he didn't come out and give the youngsters any money, or any handout of food or drink, so they kept going almost all night long, and a bunch of the rowdies from the roundhouse came and joined them. The mayor talks about stopping that kind of thing by hiring a special police to guard the houses of newlyweds the first evening," Mr. Scott said.

Mr. Jenkins laughed boisterously. "Perhaps he was too busy taking care of what she wanted . . ." he joked, and then added, "serves him right though. He's too pompous. If he hadn't inherited a fortune from his father he'd never get one cent out of what he could do for himself. The old man's death last year just pushed him into the presidency of the bank, and the staff the old man had already keeps things going. He hadn't better try pulling any high society bunk in a town like this. It's too full of tough youngsters, and they won't respect his airs. No special police has ever been able to handle any of the gangs when they get started on Halloween night, I notice."

"You're right about him, I believe. It's a shame he lets that idiot brother of his, Dick, hang around the streets of the town to be a butt for the jokes of all the boys. It might be actually dangerous. You can never know what an idiot will do or when he may turn violent. We townspeople ought to insist that he be put in a sanatorium if young Warden, or the rest of the family, haven't enough feeling about it."

"Queer thing, that idiot. I've heard there's been an idiot in that family for the last three generations—as long back as anybody in town remembers."

"Yes, every town has to have its drunkard, its idiot, its gossip, and its crook, I suppose. We are doubling up on most of those in this town. Better though that our best families should produce them so that we can have an aristocracy of the degenerate," Mr. Scott said ironically. After a silence he spoke again: "I'll be taking my family into a lake resort country for a month's outing soon, and I'll be glad to be away myself. I don't know but what I won't move to the city or to some other town within a year or so myself, when I've finished my term as postmaster. Of course for the boy, or if I should want to try politics—which I don't feel called to at the moment—or if he should later on—it would probably be best if we stayed in this community. All towns are pretty much alike I suppose, but this year I feel as if I'd had too much of it. I hear too much of the inside stories of family lives. It would surprise you if I'd tell you of some of the wives and husbands in this town who've consulted me on divorces or separations. What is it all coming to?"

Doctor Jekyll and Mr. Hyde was playing at the Grand Theatre, and ten-year-old Lloyd Toppen was going to see it with his sister, Elsie.

Mrs. Toppen, never having read the book, and having seen but few plays in her life, had no misgivings about letting the children see the play. She didn't believe that a mere play could hurt any child, and if, as Mrs. Scott suggested, it frightened them a bit, it would be a good thing to teach them to get over foolish fears; furthermore the editor of the *Weekly Eagle* had given Lloyd the tickets, so surely it couldn't be a bad play for Lloyd to see. Buxom-framed, phlegmatically goodnatured, Mrs. Toppen wasn't a woman to worry much. Nevertheless at the last moment before the children started to the theatre she said:

"I really believe I won't let you go to that horrible play. At your age going to plays! Remember you have to come home alone because father won't want to come and get you, and there's no chance the older children will want to bother."

This brough forth a great wail from both children, so Mrs. Toppen acquiesced, as she had intended doing from the beginning. Their absence would give her a little peace for one night.

"Go then but don't expect any sympathy from me if you're frightened. It will teach you to take your mother's advice if you are scared a little."

When the two children got to the theatre they separated, as Elsie saw Dolly Simpson and Lucille Gay, and went to sit with them. Lloyd, upon that, went up to the front row to sit with ten or twelve other boys he knew, and he was glad, he didn't want to sit around all evening with any sister so's you could notice it.

So long as the play was being seen with a number of others around his own age Lloyd guessed he could stand whatever happened as well as the rest of them. When the first act was over they sat clamoring about it, some sceptical as to its probability, and others sure that everything could happen just as it was going to happen. Eddie Slack, who'd read the book, told all the others the plot, and swore he'd heard of worse things in real life than that, or there wouldn't be jails and crazy houses.

"Huh," Lloyd grunted at him then, "that's just cause you're Catholic. You think that thing you got around your neck will save your life because the priest says so. I'll bet you you wouldn't get under the ice though, and let me sit over the hole you got under through. You wouldn't think it'd save you then."

Eddie however didn't feel in the mood for a sectarian discussion at the moment. All the boys were keyed up tremendously when Mr. Hyde was tossing and fuming around the stage like a mad gorilla. His body was horribly distorted; he foamed at the mouth, used his hands like claws, and sent thrills of horror through them all, as slowly but surely the discovery was made that the murderous Mr. Hyde, and Dr. Jekyll were one and the same man. After the play Lloyd lingered to talk about the man who'd acted the main part, and he agreed that you couldn't understand how a man could change himself so much as the man acting that part had. Soon the theatre was empty, but for a few stragglers. Lloyd turned to find Elsie. She was gone. She'd gone on home with Dolly Simpson, who lived near them. Lloyd was frightened. He didn't want to walk home in the dark alone now, but looking around he saw that there wasn't a boy who lived near him. Waiting outside the door to see if there wasn't somebody going his way he noticed Mr. Garner talking to two other men, and decided that he'd follow Mr. Garner, who lived a block past his house. It was some minutes before Mr. Garner left the other men and started off, and Lloyd was too shy to speak to him, but he walked behind him several paces.

It was four blocks to Lloyd's house. The first two and a half blocks he felt safe, until he noticed that Mr. Garner, who walked quickly with great long strides, was far ahead of him. Then a panic of terror came into Lloyd. He wondered if that surely was Mr. Garner ahead of him, and then in the darkness it seemed that he couldn't see Mr. Garner's form anymore; he could not be sure, it was so black dark. And there was a ditch a half block from the house he'd have to pass too. Supposing too that Mr. Garner, whom he didn't know very well, had two persons in him like Dr. Jekyll and Mr. Hyde.

This last thought put a terror into Lloyd's mind that made him walk slowly, so as to get further behind Mr. Garner. He'd wait under the light of the next street lamp to catch breath, though what if Mr. Garner didn't walk on, but hid in the ditch; or if Mr. Garner didn't do that, there might be somebody else hiding who'd jump out at lılıı.

The night seemed peopled with fearful possibilities; human devils, and unthinkable forms that might get him. There weren't only Mr. Hydes; there were ghosts, and ghouls, and wildcats, and boogie men, who would kidnap him. Standing under a dimly lit street lamp he felt safer for a moment, but still there were the trees about, and he couldn't know who might be hiding behind the trunks of those trees, and he couldn't know that they were afraid of the light, because they'd know that nobody would hear him cry out at this hour of the night. But he felt safer than away from the lamppost.

It was still a long block home, but Lloyd wanted to get there quick now. He thought he'd better sing or whistle to show that he wasn't afraid, but no sound came out of him. Going to the middle of the road to be as far away from the ditch as possible when he passed it, he started to run as fast as he could, and that was so fast that before he'd run the block he could taste his own lungs like ink within him, but he didn't dare stop running. Arriving at the porch of his house he stopped short, wanting much to break right into the door so as to be in the house with someone of the family, but a shame was in him. They'd know he was afraid if they heard him breathing so heavily. He couldn't wait long however to catch his breath, ashamed as he was. Within ten seconds, he dared not wait longer, he went in, attempting to breathe as normally as possible.

"I suppose you've come in as frightened about that silly play as Elsie was," Mrs. Toppen said. "You foolish children. Why didn't you stay together instead of the two of you coming on home alone."

"Ah I wasn't scared," Lloyd boasted. "And if I was, what good would Elsie be; she'd just make a fellow more scared than he was."

"Well, you're home now; and it's way past your bedtime. Off

you go at once. No nonsense now. You're not afraid to go up to your room alone, are you?"

"No mamma," Lloyd stuttered—"but—it was cold last night in my bed, mamma. Won't you give me another cover?"

Mrs. Toppen smiled. "That's it, is it? Come on then sonny. I see through you all right. Telling your mother you were cold in bed this season of the year with all those covers on your bed."

In the block back of the Toppens lived Mrs. James with her children. It should be said Mrs. James lived with her children because Mr. James had for years devoted his life and energies, once deemed brilliant with possibilities, to drunkenness.

The Thanksgiving season the year past Mrs. James called upon Mrs. Toppen a few days before Thanksgiving. With her appearance at the front door Mrs. Toppen scented some purpose other than a mere social visit in the call, but she was disposed to be friendly towards Mrs. James, knowing how much she had to put up with. It developed that Mrs. James had an idea about their two families having Thanksgiving dinner together, thus sharing expenses, and also being able to have a better meal and a larger gaiety.

Mrs. Toppen was not averse to this arrangement, as she felt sure that Mrs. James could manage to have her husband sober for that meal; however the Toppen children weren't keen as none of them had friends amongst the James children. Nothing came of the suggestion because no one seemed to take a decisive attitude about it one way or the other.

In years past Mrs. James had been considered quite the society lady of the town; and even yet no one doubted her gentility.

Twenty years back Wilfred J. James had come, a newly fledged young attorney from an eastern university, and set up in Wentworth. Within three months he was spoken of as one of the most brilliant minded men, regardless of age, in the State of North

Dakota. When arguing a case for a client he was dressed in morning dress, striped trousers, a morning coat, and while on the street, a stovepipe hat. His slight form had an elegance unusual for that epoch and community. Beneath his purple black hair, a white face of large and clear cut features and amazingly large, bright, and gentle eyes, revealed him as a man of extraordinary intelligence and sensibility. Many a woman in town was disappointed for her marriageable daughter when he imported a woman from the east for his wife.

Ellen James—no one knew her maiden name as she'd married him in her home town—arrived in town with a wardrobe such as the Wentworth community of that day had never gazed upon. To ladies calling upon her some days after her settling into the house which Wilfred had bought, she seemed frailly waxen, and perhaps a little too precisely aristocratic in her bearings. It proved soon however that she was capable as well as daintily made, for within a month she was singing solos Sunday at the First Presbyterian Church, and accompanied for all hymn singing. When special occasions came around she arranged programs to be given by the young people in town. An Easter cantata had never been given in Wentworth until her arrival, but concerts became frequent afterwards since she encouraged many a young person to take music lessons, or to have their voices trained.

Mrs. James had also introduced tea receptions to Wentworth in those years past, and other ladies going from her weekly affairs would comment, "It is a fine thing to have a husband who thinks so much of you, and grants you your every wish. Dear me though, I would never have time to indulge in so much social life. I would feel that I were neglecting my husband's home and my children."

On the occasions of Mrs. James' entertainments in those years Mr. James appeared at times too, and did not stand around street corners with other men as other husbands did. He was a model husband; so chivalrous and considerate; and handsome in a delicate sad way; there was something a little distrait in his manner, as there was in that of Mrs. James, too distant to suit most Wentworth inhabitants. The Jameses doubtlessly held themselves higher than ordinary people.

Five years had not passed after the marriage of Mr. James however before it was whispered that he was not using his brilliant talents to a good end. It was known that he drank, and not sociably. He was a secret drinker. Possibly nevertheless he'd control that to an extent.

Twelve more years went by. It was evident that Mr. James would never utilize his talents to make himself a power in the community. There were doubts that he made a living for the family, though nobody knew for sure whether Mrs. James had an income of her own. Now she dressed much less pretentiously than she had upon her advent into the village. She wore tailored suits, that while neat, became almost threadbare before she discarded them. It could be observed that her gloves were mended and re-mended, but she never went without gloves. It was quite a ceremony for her to put them on correctly, beginning with the fingers which she pushed down one by one; then slipping the thumb into the thumb of the glove with an efficient gesture.

As choir leader she still believed it her privilege to arrive later than other choir members. Walking down the aisle she bore herself as though conscious of a superior quality. By this time, as she was mother of four children, she'd given up playing the church organ since housework had stiffened her fingers, there having been no maid in her household for the last ten years. Mrs. Fayre, a younger woman, had proved herself a more capable pianist too, as she also had come from the East since Mrs. James' arrival.

Nevertheless Mrs. James was still a symbol of culture in town to an extent, and nobody could hold her responsible for her husband's shortcomings, though people suspected that he'd never been happy in his home life. Mrs. James was probably too demanding, without an understanding of what a man might want of a woman. Prominent people from the outside who visited the town however, were still apt to be entertained at Mrs. James' home, if only for tea, or at an evening affair where but scant refreshments were served. Concert singers, visiting politicians, and rich relatives of other people in town, were permitted to see through Mrs. James—and now through Mrs. Fayre too—that Wentworth was not lacking its people of education and refinement. Mrs. James was the one person who could surely be depended upon however to keep more or less open house if the need arose.

The James children consisted of one girl, the eldest child, and three boys. Lura, a gypsy looking girl of sixteen years, had more get up and go to her than the other children seemed to have. She'd been born before Mr. James drank so much as to have weakened his constitution. Two of the boys, Frederick and William Henry— Mrs. James always wanted her children called by their full names, as she thought nicknames vulgar—were nice looking, dark-skinned boys, with well bred manners that had nothing of the girlboy in them; but they never chummed much with other boys in town which probably saved them from being dubbed sissies. The other boys did not dislike them, but they were not much fun to play with because they obeyed their mother's too strict dictates absolutely.

However, Lloyd Toppen was friendly enough with the younger of these two boys, William Henry, whom Lloyd called Billy when Mrs. James was not around. He knew about the times that Mr. James came home intoxicated. Billy did not remember the first time that happened, but his sister Lura had told him. She said Mrs. James had been frightened of her husband, though he was mild enough in his drunkenness. The next day he was abject; he never got over being shamefaced about his weakness, but by now it was a rare week that Mr. James wasn't completely intoxicated once or twice, and sometimes for days at a time.

William Henry James was a strange boy, though he was more apt to cut up and be a good pal for other boys his age than his older brother; and his younger brother was just a pretty four-year-old with curly black hair. Weird streaks of sullenness came over William Henry at a moment's notice though, and he would then be impossible to play with, or if he did come around within a minute

30

or so and act decent again, you could never tell when he'd trip you up, or try to scratch you on some silly grudge. At other times however he couldn't be nice enough about sharing candy he had, or helping with a chore.

William Henry sang out loud at school, and it was an even match between him and Lloyd Toppen as to which had the best boy soprano voice, except that Lloyd did not have any quaver in his voice. For that matter William Henry didn't have a real quaver in his, when he sang without knowing that anybody was listening. He no doubt thought that quavers in the voice were extra exquisite qualities because when his mother sang her voice quavered too.

Generally upon Sunday nights William Henry would walk home with his mother from church, and this while the other youngsters in town, if they could sneak away from under their parents' watchful eyes, were tearing about playing run-sheep-run, pump-pump pull-away, or other games.

One Sunday night however Mrs. James couldn't find William Henry when she looked for him upon coming out of church, until her eye discerned him walking away with Hazel Fisher. She was put out somewhat, but smiled, not wanting to be hard on his boyish admiration for Hazel, which he had revealed to her by his conversation. The next day at school some boys teased him about Hazel being his girl. He was pleased at first, and even courted further teasing, until some boy taunted him with the statement that Hazel was not his girl really.

"She likes Lloyd Toppen better than she does you; she's just stringing you along."

William Henry became morose upon this and sulked about most of the day, so much that he was teased more, now that other boys saw how easily he was upset. For several days he was not to be approached because he was so sulky; then, one night when about fifteen children were playing hunt-the-fox all around the six blocks of the neighborhood, William Henry came around, making the others think for the moment that he'd become goodnatured again, and was ready to play with them, though some of them suggested that they run away from him as he wasn't liked. One game had just been finished so that everybody was standing near the tennis court that was the goal, wondering if it was too dark to start another game. Just as Lloyd Toppen was going to call out to William Henry and tell him to come and play he stopped short in front of them and struck a dramatic posture. The others wondered what he was up to now, and Carey Framer was ready to tease him, until an older girl said:

"Aw, you've teased him enough. Let him alone. I guess you wouldn't like to have everybody teasing you for several days either, would you?"

Just then William Henry, who had halted sharply and was standing very erect about fifteen feet from the others, put up his hand and shouted out in an intense voice, that wasn't fooling at all, "Lloyd Toppen, are you there?"

Lloyd stepped out, wanting to be friendly to Billy whom he'd had some nice times with when they were both feeling lonely, with nobody else to play with. He started to say something to try and make Billy not act sulky any more, when William Henry shouted out again, in as terrific a voice as he could, "Halt."

Lloyd, wondering what Billy was up to now, stopped, remembering that he and some others had been thinking that Billy was queer in his head. William Henry shouted out again, "Lloyd Toppen, step forward and I will charge."

Lloyd didn't know what to do. He felt sheepish, and he didn't want to fight Billy, because Billy was too serious about it, and wouldn't fight fair anyway. Besides if he wasn't right in his head—

Someone amongst the other children hooted, and laughed, ridiculing Billy.

"Ah go home, you William Henry James. This ain't no tournament. You're off yer nut. The only charge there is in your family is the charging your ma does at stores on bills she don't pay."

"You mean thing," Carey Framer told the boy who'd spoken up.

"Come on Billy," Lloyd Toppen said, going up to him. "It wasn't me that said that. I haven't done anything to you, and I can't help it if them other darn fools tease you. If you like Hazel Fisher I'm telling you she's nothing to me, and I'm nothing to her. Those fellows just see that it teases you to say that."

William Henry was silently sulky. Then he kicked at Lloyd, who'd reached out to touch him on the shoulder, but he didn't persist after the first kick. Instead he turned and ran home.

After that day William Henry wouldn't play around with any of the children; and his brother Frederick couldn't get him to play with him even. He'd skulk about town, cross if anybody tried to be friendly with him.

At about this time Mr. James had taken to being intoxicated for such long periods that he'd been blacklisted at every saloon in town; all grocery stores had been informed by Mrs. James that they must sell him nothing whatever; and particularly not vanilla or extracts that he'd taken to drinking for what alcohol there was in them. Thus driven, he'd been known once to climb into a freight car and break open a box containing bottles of vanilla; that night he'd been found lying in the street near his home, unable to get home alone. Another night he was found in the same condition on the road outside town, and later it was discovered that he'd obtained alcohol by draining juice from a corn silo. This liquor was powerful with raw alcohol. Once having discovered that source of drink one could know that Mr. James wouldn't live long unless he was in some way stopped. By now however it looked as though it would be a mercy for all concerned if he would pass out as soon as possible.

Mr. James was still under forty-five years of age; when sober and well dressed, he could yet present a distinguished front to the town, though his brooding eyes were shifty with the shame of his weakness, and fogged gray rather than black through long excess. The whiteness of his face in sober moments was deathmasklike; his high white forehead seemed covered with a parchment skin upon which fine perspiration would show at the slightest exertion on his part. His once sensitively formed mouth sagged and trembled uncontrollably. He was completely a wreck that went furtively amongst the streets of Wentworth and through the doorways of his own home.

One day, after having been unable for several days to get anything in the form of alcohol to drink, Mr. James was sitting in his messed up office, for the moment not possessed of a great yearning for drink. He dazedly reviewed his past, all of the panorama of which was dim as a badly projected moving picture to his consciousness. He wondered if he had actual regrets about it; if he cared enough about anything in life for that. He ought, he mused, to be sorry for his wife and his children, but reflected too that he'd never wanted them. They had never come to mean more to him than children that he saw about his house. Never that he could remember had there been in him a consistent will to accomplish some definite thing; only the vague ecstatic decision to conquer that he'd had in youth. His marriage had taken place more as a convention conceded to than as a result of desire. Thinking back over acquaintances of the past, his colleagues in Wentworth and elsewhere, he couldn't find in himself a wish that he had acted and become as they had.

What the impulse was that made some men so contented, apparently, with material success, and in the having of a home and family, he did not know. Plainly of course, he and his wife had never cared for each other except with a removed respect; strange that; that a man and woman could consort together for years, and be the parents of children and yet seem strangers to each other. Strange too that he'd not once since his college days been able to feel affectionately companionable to any of his fellow men; but that was explainable in a way by the few young men, or men of any mentality there had been in Wentworth the first years of his life there. He recalled younger, expectant days—and dreams he used to have then. The dream of flying, pursued by a mob which never could catch him, and in the dream he would run up the sky, and down, and up again, taunting the people who pursued him. The dream of finding piles of money in the sand too, and so many piles that he never could take any one pile, because all about were other and larger piles of money that slipped from his hand, overflowing. His dream-life was different now; a region of desolate and grotesque events, but not so desolate and grotesque as his waking life, he believed. If he could weep? But no, he could not even feel misused or pursued—only despairing, tired in the pit of his stomach, intensely so. How steel cold and clear his intellect cut out for him a picture of all life as futile.

As he thought, he wanted to drink and so to escape thinking; that wish was probably the main strain of his yearning for drink, and it met no obstacles in his will because his sober mind did not point out to him now, and had not for years pointed out, a more enviable condition than that of drunkenness.

Three nights later, after Mrs. James had been worrying slightly about her husband's absence, though she was used to his being gone for days at a time, Wilfred James was found dead on the bank of the creek which flowed through Harold Park in the center of town. He'd apparently stumbled from the bridge to lie down upon the bank while staggering home the night before, and sleeping in a drunken stupor, had simply passed on into the stiller darkness of complete and irrevocable unconsciousness. He was handsome in death; which in its beauty had tensified his dissipated face. The parchment mask was calm, as if never written upon except by peace.

Soon after her husband's death Mrs. James began to talk of going to Canada to take a claim. It was only essential that she have money to fall back upon in her pioneering efforts, and perhaps, she discussed with her eighteen year old daughter, Lura, money would be forthcoming, now that Lura finished the Normal School in a few months, and could teach school at a fair salary. With what money Mrs. James had, and help from Lura of a few dollars a month, she believed that life in Canada could be managed, as Frederick and William Henry were both old enough to work at cultivating a few acres of the farm claim.

While waiting for Lura's graduation Mrs. James decided to take boarders, and thereby add to her scanty capital. However the only person who came to stay with her was Miss Snow, a new, and the youngest, teacher at Central High School.

Miss Snow was a large girl, with pale smooth beauty and an evidently quiet disposition. For a girl of but twenty years she was remarkably poised and mature minded, as she must naturally have been to have finished a university course and to have taken a degree in that time. The first week she was in town she went to the livery stable and arranged to have a riding horse brought to the James house every morning at seven, so that she could have an hour's canter before breakfasting and going to the high school to teach. Within two weeks however Mr. Doll refused to send any of his horses to her as she always brought them back trembling with exhaustion and covered with sweat. He'd seen how she rode them; full gallop always, and lashing them mercilessly if they relaxed.

This angered Miss Snow, who, coming from a city where she was used to many people about, and a variety of ways to amuse herself, felt miserably cooped up in Wentworth. What young men there were who lived in town and who might be acceptable companions to her were away at college, or were employed in positions out of town, since no young man with life in him would stay and petrify in Wentworth. As she went up and down Egan Avenue at times it infuriated her when she realized that men standing about the poolhall, or the drugstore, commented on her, or on any woman, as she passed.

She repelled advances made to her by any of them to be friendly, even though they might be presented to her in a manner deemed respectable. Now that she couldn't have her morning rides, with an all day jaunt into the country on Saturdays and Sundays, she did not know what to do with her spare time, as readable books were scarcely procurable. Plainly she was not going to do as many girls her age in town did, meet trains to pick up travelling men. Her position as teacher would not permit that, if her pride would, but she had already a preconceived contempt for the entire species of travelling salesmen who came through this section of the country, boasting to each other no doubt, wherever they went, of the ease with which they picked up, carried on flirtations with, and even had sexual relationships with, the best class girls in the towns they visited.

Seventeen-year-old Clarence Toppen was in the senior history class which Miss Snow taught, and he was popular amongst his high school companions because of his football prowess, though of course this very prowess made him the victim of jealousy amongst other boys in town. However his goodnatured softness—mushiness, his older sisters called it—made him a target for girls' attentions, because he could be easily manipulated. At the moment most of his attentions were being directed at Lillian Thompson, a fluffy blond doll of a girl, whose confiding babyisms and willingness to cuddle appeased his puppy sexual affectionateness.

Miss Snow occasionally encountered Clarence on the streets and they would fall into step together as they lived in the same direction. He amused her; he was somebody to talk to, and was amiably ready to do whatever he could for her, like trying to locate a riding horse, or suggesting means for her to pass time away. One night as he was passing the James house he saw her in the hammock on the porch, and went up to say good evening. Once there he lingered.

The dusk deepened; the evening air was mild, sentimentally so. With a fearsomely audacious move Clarence seated himself in the hammock with Miss Snow, who appeared to think nothing of the move. He felt her feminine presence, and a thrill at being accepted as a companion, as a suitor almost, by this older and beautiful woman, warmed his whole being. It occurred to him that Miss Snow was the most beautiful woman he'd ever seen in his life; her ivory pallor of skin, which was a healthy pallor; her strangely distant grey eyes; her softly gleaming fawn-coloured hair; and her large but well made body clad always in garments that were to him the last thing in fashion, gave her a romantic aura.

Seated in the hammock Clarence found his body thrust closely to that of Miss Snow, and she gave no evidence of removing herself from the contact. At moments it even came into his mind that she was gently leaning against him. Dared he put his arm about her? The question thrilled him for several moments, as darkness was drifting all around them. He talked to her sympathetically about the dullness of Wentworth, and what a shame it was she should have to be spending her time there simply to make a living as a teacher. He was sure she was pressing herself closer to him. He did not know what to do with his hand. Then Miss Snow leaned forward, and spoke softly.

"You're a dear boy, Clarence," she murmured, and took his face in her hands as she put her lips to his. He was taken aback at the first moment, and then put his arms about her and responded with a kiss.

"I've been so lonely. I'm being silly, and I'm so much older too," Miss Snow said, but held him closer to her.

"Only three years," Clarence whispered huskily, feeling panicky, but feeling also the conquering male. But he did not know what more to say, because he was sure she'd think him ridiculous if he talked baby talk and mush to her, as he talked it to Lillian. But there was no need to speak.

"Let's walk; away from this porch where the James family might be seeing us," Miss Snow suggested.

As they went down the walk William Henry James passed them. Seeing Clarence with Miss Snow a dark look went over his face; he always felt sullen if he saw Miss Snow talking to a man or boy, though he hardly dared speak to her himself.

William Henry had just reached the age of fourteen shortly after his father's death. The age, a difficult one, was more so for him because of his temperament, and his consciousness of what people must feel about his family. With strange moods that came upon him, a distrust of people, and a sense that people were thinking he was not normal, he'd become a skulking figure, isolated from all school comrades.

Soon after she'd retired to bed a little after eleven o'clock Miss Snow heard a rapping on her window. Immediately she was stinging with a nearly instinctive fear from her distrust of this small city in the midst of a prairie wilderness. Reaching from her bed to the bureau near it, she opened the drawer and fumbled about until her hand grasped a small revolver she kept there. Within a moment a leg appeared through the open window, and then an entire body.

"Stop or I will shoot," Miss Snow called out sharply, but the figure kept moving into the room through the window, so that nervously she pressed the trigger of her revolver, and the body fell backwards out of the window, making a dull thud as it fell to the ground one story below. An intuition, come from she knew not where within herself, that the body which she had shot was that of William Henry James, was in her.

Her intuition was right. The shot which had caused him to fall had not killed him however. It had only scathed him, and the shock of the report had caused him to fall from fright more than had the bullet wound. Mrs. James, having heard the shot, rushed outside and soon was followed by Miss Snow in her dressing gown.

William Henry refused to talk, and maintained his sullen silence for several days, through which days a movement on the part of some people in town caused him to be sentenced to the State Boys' Reformatory School. Once the story of his having attempted to break into Miss Snow's room got around, other rumours about him spread. It was said he'd attempted some atrocious thing with little Genevieve Holden, and other girls, his own age, claimed to be afraid of him.

Miss Snow, feeling sorry for William Henry, went with him the day he was being taken to the train that was to carry him to the Reform School. She declared that she thought it the wrong place to send him, if he needed to be sent anywhere. Walking beside him she heard him murmur, "my lady's balcony," under his breath, or perhaps as a part of a speech he was trying to make to her.

It was all wrong, Miss Snow felt sure, that he should be put amongst criminally inclined boys at a Reformatory, but there was nothing she could do to stop it. Perhaps after all, she concluded, if the thing which had prompted his act had been only a foolish boy's romantic idea, the promptings of his nature would not always be so little dangerous.

Not liking rumours of things said about her which began to come to her ears Miss Snow suddenly resigned her position as teacher in the high school and left town. The President of the School Board told her that she would have to give a month's notice at least, if she would not wait until after the Christmas holidays. Miss Snow, however, treated the President and his statement with impulsive disdain, and left Wentworth two days after she had told him she wished to resign.

Down in the shack in the alley back of Egan Avenue Brick Simpson was holding forth. Len Cook had managed somewhere to get hold of a quart of whiskey, and Brick supplemented this with six bottles of beer he'd swiped from a case behind the saloon. Gus Johnson and Mike Tolls played a game of craps in one corner of the room, while five other fellows were playing poker around a box used as a table. Peter Reynalds, afraid that his mother might hear he was hanging around with this set which she declared ruffianly, was standing guard, looking outside frequently, very frequently to see that the bulls did not catch them drinking, playing poker, and shooting craps. He'd never tasted whiskey in his life, but Brick who was only fourteen, joshed him about it, so he swore he'd try it. He liked Brick in spite of the fact that his mother was only a seamstress and supposed to be half dotty in her German upper story. If Brick had a chance like other fellows in town, Peter thought, he'd have been the brightest fellow about. As it was he was the best swimmer and scrapper of his age, and he was always first when it came to swiping oranges and peanuts from the Greek candy store, or pies from the bakery.

Gene Collins, and Lloyd Scott, were more nervous even than Peter, because as they were of small families, their mothers checked up on them more than Peter's did on him. Gene swore he wouldn't drink either beer or whiskey because he didn't like the taste, and Lloyd defended that there wasn't any use trying to do something you don't like just to be smart-alecky.

"Ah, for God's sake," Brick Simpson swore, "youse guys are damn fraid cats. You ought not to come away from your mammas. I'll bet you'd be afraid to put it into a girl even if she ast you. If you can't take a little sip of whiskey, or beer at least, you don't need to try and make me think you did anything to them White girls the other night up in the hayloft," he abused Gene and Peter. "They've got more guts than you have."

"Who wants doing anything to fat things like them; they are almost as bad as their greasy dad who nearly got strung up last year for trying to start something with a fourteen-year-old girl," Len Cook said, at the moment trying to be friendly to Peter, Gene, and Lloyd. Len's parents were in bad odour in town, and he knew from his older sisters that they didn't like that because it'd ruin their chances of marrying. Besides Len had just missed being sent to the reform school a few months back for stealing a watch from the Smith Jewelry store. All the youngsters in town, except the dead-heads, were ready to steal fruit, food, candy, and such things, but none of them so far as they knew of each other, had ever taken anything so valuable as a watch.

Bull Norton, from the roundhouse, drifted into the shack looking for Gus Johnson. His presence made the boys uneasy as he was blustery and bullying. Even Brick was afraid Bull would find he had a quart of whiskey and take it away from him.

"What in the name of Jesus Christ are you runts hanging around here for? It's hard enough to find a hangout in this burg without making a kindergarten out of this joint. Beat it," Bull Norton said roughly after a minute, showing he was in a black mood. Gus Johnson, delivery wagon clerk from Harm's grocery store, spoke up saying, "Ah, let the kids alone. They keep an eye out don't you worry. These kids ain't softies."

"To hell with them."

"You don't own the place I guess," Peter said, feeling himself backed up by the other youngsters, and a little by Gus Johnson, whom he knew though would never actually buck Bull Norton.

"What's that?" Bull turned on Peter. "Do you want a punch on the jaw?"

Peter, quaking, but angry with dislike of Bull, backed away, answering, "Try punching me in the mouth and see what you'll get. I don't have to stand any roughstuff from you. My brother knocked hell out of you once and he can do it again if you try picking on us kids. But I wouldn't even ask him to. I'd sail a rock through you myself if you try touching me."

"What'd I say; these goddamned kids; they ought to be home being nursed by their mammas," Bull growled, but did nothing further. As everybody in the shack seemed against him but the placating Gus Johnson, he departed mumbling within a minute or two. Soon after, the six bottles of beer were opened, and consumed, every one of the boys taking some out of bravado. Then too the whiskey bottle was opened, but by this time some older men had come into the shack so that the younger boys had no chance to have more than a sip of it, which was a relief to them. It was twelve o'clock before any of them started to leave for home.

"I'll get holy Jesus from the folks if I can't slip into the house unnoticed," Lloyd Scott declared.

"Thank God, dad's out of town, and mother will be sleeping because she's going to have another kid soon. Why in the devil she's started having them after an eight year wait I don't know, but that'll mean two squallers around our house now," Gene Collins said.

"I'll get hell and there's no chance of my not," Peter Reynalds said, "because my old woman always sits up and waits for me."

"Lets you and me go down to the Normal School and hie rocks at some windows in the dormitory there," Brick Simpson suggested to Peter. "You'll get hell anyway, so you might as well stick out a little longer. There may be some girls that will climb down the fire escape and come down to fuss awhile. I know a couple who'll really give a guy a little humping if you coax'em enough and they're feeling hot."

After some persuasion Peter agreed to this suggestion, and saying good night to Gene and Lloyd, started down the street with Brick.

A great scandal was on in town which involved the sons and daughters of the most prominent families. It had first started by it being discovered that the young men of the town were gambling and drinking their idle hours away in the shack at the end of the alley back of Egan Avenue. The matron of the Normal School dormitory too, glancing from her window one night, saw two young ladies descending from their rooms via fire escape, into the arms of town boys; going to various rooms she discovered who the ladies absent were, and it was not until five o'clock in the morning that they returned again. Immediately these girls, Estelle Lockwood, and Lola Howard, were threatened with expulsion, but the expulsion did not take place as Estelle's father was a United States senator, and a man of much power in the State. It seemed, from the story, that the girls climbed from their windows to chat with town boys, and were later picked up by older young men in an automobile. There was but one thing to think when they did not come in until morning.

And Gene Collins and Peter Reynalds had breaths that smelled of alcohol. It had been noticed by Mrs. Lewis one day as she stopped them to ask Gene how his mother was, after giving birth to a new daughter. It was believed that Leonard Cook and Brick Simpson were the ringleaders in this vicious young circle, and neither Gene nor Peter denied that they were horrible influences, though in private conversation with Lloyd Scott, whose name happened not to be mixed up with the story, they agreed that neither Len nor Brick ever did much actually but follow-on in an attempt to be a part of the more select group of young men in town. They also agreed however that because of parents it was best to let it

43

appear that these two were the evil influences in their lives, as Brick and Len never got hell from their parents so severely as they got from theirs.

Close on top of this scandal, which soon involved discussion on the morals of all the younger generation, came another. No girl was immune from the suggestion of being fast if she consorted at all with men; no young man was there but what it was thought went to the house of ill fame three miles from town. And now the singer who'd stayed over in town when Dr. Miller, evangelist, had departed after wholesaledly converting two thirds of the town populace, was in for trouble. Real trouble.

Alfred Bingham, before his conversion, had been a wild young man of twenty-six, who lived in a city miles from Wentworth. He'd thought to become an opera singer, and then Dr. Miller got hold of him and led him into the paths of righteousness, so that he accompanied the doctor in his evangelizing travels, and was official hymn leader in all the towns that Dr. Miller visited, spreading the rapid fire gospel. Alfred, curly haired, six feet tall, and broadshouldered, would stand on the platform, and his rich baritone vibrated through the entire huge, barnlike, newly-erected conversion hall, as he sang the first verse and refrain of each hymn before leading the assembly in their rendition of it.

It's the old time religion
the old time religion
the old time religion
is good enough for me.

His voice would boom forth fervourously, as his violet eyes gleamed and his handsome young face shone with theatrical religious conviction.

After fourteen hundred people had been converted, Alfred Bingham decided upon the departing date of Dr. Miller, that he would give up the roving life and settle in Wentworth as singing teacher. He soon became one of the most popular young men who'd ever

44

been in town. There was no telling what girl he might marry. It looked as though Mary Warden, banker's heiress, had succumbed.

Then the past came rushing to meet, or to catch Alfred Bingham. It appeared that he was wanted in another county for mayhem—the meaning of the word nobody knew on first hearing, but this ignorance was not long lived.

In the outskirts of Perryville, the village that had been Alfred Bingham's boyhood town, there lived a lady of some fifty years of age. By her house once every week or so a travelling grocer went with his wagonload of provisions. He had done this for some years, dispensing groceries and drygoods to farm and village women. The house of this lady had been on these trips a convenient resting place for a night for the elderly pedlar; it had been so for a long time and the rumour was that the relationship between these two elderly people was not a chaste one.

Alfred Bingham, after being converted to the one and only true faith by Dr. Miller, visited his home town, previous to embarking upon his hymn leading career with the doctor. Rumours of the relationship between these two elderly people came to his ear, and in his newly begotten religious fervour he was revolted, indignant. He couldn't talk sufficiently of how disgusting the old man and woman were. And one night, a rainy one, in passing the poolhall of Perryville, he encountered two townsmen and former pals of his, both rather lit up with drink. Then Alfred slipped a little; he talked of their behavior and how he was he also

"I'll tell you boys, we ought to go and see if the old man is there tonight, and if he is, nut him. He's old enough so he ought to cut out playing with the women by now," Slim Adams said jokingly. "Though of course we all stay a little hot between the legs until they pile dirt upon us."

Alfred Bingham, drunk, and earnest with Christian zeal, did not take the remark so jokingly as it was made; he argued, and insisted that the three of them go to the old lady's house to see if the pedlar was there, so the three of them started off. They arrived at the house and knocked; after an interval the old grocery pedlar came to the door, in his nightshirt, holding a lamp, looking aged, and frightened. Without further parley the three young men laid strong hands on him and carried him kicking and protesting into a woodshed back of the old lady's house. There upon the workbench Alfred Bingham performed the operation of castration, with a jackknife that he carried in his pocket. Then, suddenly sober, affrighted by what they had done, the three young men left, and took the midnight train out of town.

It was only now, six months later, that Alfred Bingham was located in connection with this act, which had caused the death of the old grocery pedlar. At any rate Alfred Bingham was taken by the authorities from Wentworth to stand trial for something he'd done, whether the mayhem story was the true report or not. No one actually knew, and there was church influence to keep the story quiet so as to prevent further backsliding after the glorious evangelical success of Dr. Miller.

It was regrettable this, because there were enough rebellious souls ready to backslide from the true religion in Wentworth as it was. Even Mrs. Lewis had little to say—though she mumbled an idea she never had mumbled while Dr. Miller was in town—that getting religion by conversion through evangelism had its defects.

Mr. Scott, and Mr. Collins—the latter particularly, as he was a railroad engineer and used to knocking about—were inclined to be easy in their attitudes towards their sons in the storm of rumours that were about regarding what the young people of between fourteen and twenty years of age were doing. Mr. Scott was not so sure; but Mr. Collins knew that a few wild oats have to be sown in youth. In fact he never got his own completely planted in those young years. But Mr. Scott, more austere, was lenient because he was fairly sure that his son Lloyd never departed far from under the watchful eye of his wife Margaret. Still he hastened the departure of his family for a vacation into a lake resort country, and they were gone six weeks, by which time much talk had quieted down, since the normal school vacation came on but three weeks after the girls' dormitory scandal. Allen Jenkins moved with his father and his new stepmother to Minneapolis. He'd never been involved in much of the gossip except that Mrs. Lewis had felt it necessary to inform his father that he was seen walking through Harold Park one evening with his arm about Fritzie Hammer's waist. Events became so dull in the town with the increasing heat of the summer months, the closing of all schools, and the departure of many townspeople for visits and vacations, that the whole world seemed stagnating to what few young people remained. There was only one interlude, the Chautauqua season, and it this year was a dull season, as the lake had nearly dried up for some reason no one knew much about. The hot, dusty, summer days, dragged on; finally autumn and the re-opening of the Normal and city schools occurred again, and with this, social life started anew with as much impetus as it ever had.

Hunting season came along; and around the marshes some miles out of town various men and boys put up their screens, for the shooting of wild duck; or men wandered across prairies covered with high dried weeds, to scare up prairie chicken. In the clear luminousness of autumn air there was invigoration. Prairie dog villages would be passed; and before the inhabitants of these villages scurried to their holes on the approach of a man or men, they would stand alert, listening; and as soon as the human beings had passed they would be out of their holes again, standing sentinel at their dirt-heap houses, and barking back and forth at each other challenges and prairie dog society greetings.

Many a prairie chicken stood alert to listen, poised for flight, just a moment too long. That season was a great one for sportsmen. Almost every day hunters would come in with wild duck, quail, or chicken—as many as forty to a man in some cases.

Glenn Warden was back from college, having graduated in June. He was finding it hard to spend the three summer months in

Wentworth before going to Chicago, as he intended, to start working—at something. Indecision about what this would be also bothered him. All of the boys he'd known in Wentworth he'd either grown away from, or they had left town. Erik Watson was in Sioux Falls with an older, established attorney; Sam Reynalds had a sales manager's job in Saint Paul with a shoe house; Tom Granger was away up in Alaska; and Bill Cook, in town yet, was impossible as a companion for Glenn now. He had nothing to talk about but women, and woman chasing.

Awareness that he need do nothing so far as having enough money to live on was concerned did not ease his mind; in spite of the income of a fortune which his father had left him, with his brothers and sisters, he felt he would be a despicable figure in America not doing something. It was too bad he hadn't taken up law; or medicine; then at least he'd still be in college with the question of selecting a life work not an immediate one.

Added to his unrest about work, and because of the dullness of life in Wentworth, was the pitying worry over his mother if she should discover how meaningless her religion, Catholicism, was to him. Already she had severed relationships with his oldest sister Mary, whom she bitterly accused of being a heretic. He regretted that. In spite of the fact that his mother's attitudes seemed to him but old world superstitions, based on fear and ignorance, he wished to seem to her faithful in his convictions yet. She was aging rapidly; and the death of her husband; the blow of Mary's departure from the church; worry about her idiot son, Dick, and his increasing imbecility, with the departure of all her children from the home and Wentworth; made her last years miserable, and isolated ones. She was bitter and hard in her fanaticism about her faith, and Glenn was unwilling to be one more cause for bitterness in her life.

He'd tried to escape his worry and unrest in various ways. Playing pool at night bored him; his attempt to become interested in Mabel Thompson was not successful. She was undoubtedly beautiful in a perfect featured, calm, dark, manner, but he found her vain, indolent, and when trying to be animated, silly. Her younger sister, Lenore, was much better with her flapperish impertinences, but Lenore was concerned with boys nearer her own age, with whom she could be more carefree, and could boss completely. An effort to read too had been a failure, for while he attempted to persuade himself that he was intent on a book, or on abstract contemplation, the dim noises of life on the streets intruded upon his consciousness, making a jagged thread of his will.

This afternoon, sitting in an arm chair, he was thinking of college, and events that had happened there. Particularly he was remembering his chief friend the last year, Ted Sanborn. What would become of him? Had he a job yet?—His father had said he'd give him no more allowance money after graduation. Reflected upon, it appeared to Glenn that all of the experience of college life had been completely fulfilled so far as human relationships were concerned, and the studies had not perturbed him. He missed the fraternity house atmosphere; the fellowship with members of his own sex. Not many of them were actually sympathetic, or intelligent, but they'd more nearly approached understanding than anybody about him at the moment. Once or twice he'd caught Mabel Thompson in a mood rare to her, when she seemed to understand some of the emotions that were in him making him restless, and also baffled about life. At these times a satisfying discussion might occur, and she'd be grave, rather than flirtatious; but the next day she'd revert. He liked the way she admitted her lack of ambition, and her lack of emotion about much of anything. She confessed that she wasn't going on with music in spite of the fact that her voice was naturally a remarkable one, simply because it meant too much work. Her trip to Europe had been a bad thing for her morale, he judged, because she perceived through it that her talents were not so remarkable, and her beauty not so amazing, as she had been led to suppose by admiration in Wentworth. What she wanted now was marriage, and Glenn judged that she was wondering if he wouldn't propose, as his income would let him marry now, and he was the only possible marriageable man about town for a girl of her outlook.

As he fretted within himself he began to feel drowsy in the sticky summer heat, and at last dozed off. A clammy vapour hovered about his consciousness as he slept. Vague visions passed through his dormant mind, oppressing him. Snatches of rational conversation were spoken between characters, and then the scene would again become incoherent. There appeared in his dream the figure of Ted Sanborn, and his presence seemed strange, not quite right. The figure approached him as he was sitting, in the dream as in fact, slumped into a chair.

"I've been looking for you, Glenn. I've wanted to talk things over with you," the figure said, and seated itself on the arm of Glenn's chair. Glenn felt uncomfortable, as though Ted ought to know it was too hot a day to sit so close. He wondered what Ted was up to. "Take my hand," the figure said, and put one arm about Glenn's shoulder, while he took Glenn's hand with his own free hand. After a moment he leaned over so that Glenn could feel the warmth of his body, and Ted's breath against his face. He stirred slightly, but felt no objection. The embrace of his friend became more firm, and his lips pressed against Glenn's, as he said passionately:

"God, God, God,—I've been so tormented wondering what was going to become of me. I can't think. I wonder if you don't understand; can't help?"

Gradually Glenn woke up. He felt dazed; his eyes seemed sticky, and covered with a mist. For almost two minutes he could not feel sure it had been a dream, the presence of Ted had been so real, and now awake, nothing about him appeared real. All was misty, mystifying, and not pleasantly so.

He couldn't think, or feel. He didn't know what to do. He knew he'd have to get out of Wentworth sooner than he had intended. Going to his room he washed, and then went out of the house to drift, revolting against the doing of it, down to the poolhall. That there was no other solution for the moment irked him. Yes, he must get away; he could do his mother no good staying in town in a continual state of mind such as possessed him now. He wondered if Ted was in Chicago by now—a letter would find out. There had to be somebody to talk to who would take him out of himself.

Prof. Lawrence was in a satisfied mood, almost purring within himself. Before him were six culprits, boys who'd climbed in through the window of the Main Normal School building, and stolen—stolen—over five hundred badges meant to be used on Labour Day. He was telling them harshly that they must each pay two dollars out of money they themselves earned, and within two days, or that he would have them sent to the reform school. His thin figure was tight with an ecstacy of henpecking rancour. His ferret-eyed, thin, ascetic face had a fanatical glow upon it, as he assured them that they would all come to bad ends.

Not in the two years since he'd been a professor at the Normal School had Mr. Lawrence so enjoyed himself. He was being guardian to justice; he was managing to terrify these young ruffians at last. They wouldn't be so inclined to titter behind his back and burlesque him as he walked down the street now; and more, the sister of one of them, Miss Hardcutt, who was a teacher in the Normal, might learn her place too. Indeed, she would take a year's sick leave from a school in Minneapolis, and believe she could teach classes previously assigned to him, while resting! She and her airs! He'd see how she liked having the screw turned in her young devil of a brother. Already he could hear her asking him to be lenient; she would not be so indifferent in her manner then. He had his reply ready.

"We must not be harsh, Miss Hardcutt, but we must be just. It's a regrettable incident, but the other children in the school are to be considered and if we let this incident pass—"

"It was this way, sir," Ben Granger stutteringly tried to explain, "some feller or other said he'd dare me to get one of the buttons to wear before they were given out, and when I took two—only two sir—the others climbed in and took one or two each. There wasn't no five hundred taken by us sir; there must of been somebody else after us."

"Five hundred there are that are missing, Benjamin," Prof. Lawrence answered.

The other five boys told the same story as Ben Granger but the professor was adamant in his decision. When the boys were finally released from his presence they went, frightened, but joking to each other in bravado.

"The devil," said Sammy Hardcutt, "I took more'n two maybe, but I darn well didn't take over ten, and neither did the rest of you. He's a darned old liar. If we took fifty we was going some because I was the last one and the box was nearly full then."

Three days later, when Labour Day came around there were a thousand buttons distributed. The order for buttons had been for twelve hundred. This fact was noted by Miss Hardcutt and commented upon. She spoke to Mr. Lawrence,

"I notice that there are a few buttons left over, Mr. Lawrence, after a thousand have been distributed; over a hundred I judge. I believe we should punish the boys but it's hardly best to exaggerate their crime. That hardens them."

Prof. Lawrence however did not retreat in his demands, but by the time a week had passed the boys' fright had worn off, and they forgot their promise to pay Mr. Lawrence two dollars each. They had heard incidentally that President Hays, of the Normal School, had been seen to conceal a smile when told of the button incident most seriously by the Professor. Apparently he wasn't going to back up the Professor's demands with great force.

As a result of the incident, Henry Jameson, the only boy who paid the Professor, was called a fraid-cat by Ben Hardcutt, and had to knock a chip off Ben's shoulder, and then there was a fistfight which never came to a decision because the boys saw Mrs. Granger coming down the street before they'd finished; and somehow they didn't feel like starting a new fight elsewhere.

Miss Randall came superciliously into the village to teach history at the Normal School. She was used to this section of the country, having grown up in a town in the Black Hills; but at sixteen she'd gone to a private girls' school in Washington, D.C., and later to Columbia University, so that now she had no expectations of meeting anybody with whom she could converse intelligently. However she discovered that Miss Hardcutt, teaching also at the Normal as a year's rest from city work, was well read and informed;—a specialist on vocational guidance and sociological research work, in a minor way.

The half term before Miss Randall's arrival Miss Hardcutt had led a very quiet life, because she had few tolerable companions, and also because she'd just had an operation the summer before for some woman's trouble. Now however she replenished her wardrobe in Minneapolis, began to give teas and parties in collaboration with Miss Randall, collected together all the possible bachelors and eligible men in town, and resolved to have as entertaining a time as possible. Neither she nor Miss Randall much desired marriage; they both had ambitions to have careers. Miss Randall wished to become a stage director and intended within a year to go to New York and get into appropriate theatre work. Miss Hardcutt had already done suffragette campaign work, and intended going on with vocational guidance work with the purpose of finding woman's place in the industrial world, and making the sex "class conscious," or "clash conscious," her brothers thought.

Early in the beginning of the new year the two, with the aid of Mrs. Hammer, managed to hold an "evening" at the First Presbyterian Church at which votes for women were discussed. Miss Hardcutt got together a group of the town's "most representative men" of talent, and believed that the ones she had gathered were to speak in favour of enfranchisement for women. She was disappointed only in Supt. May of the Central High School, who gave not even a witty talk against the cause; he fell back on the old nail "woman's place is the home."

Upon this Miss Hardcutt arose and began a speech with the comment that "Not only is woman's place often the home, but the home—a supervised one—is the place for all people, regardless of sex, deficient in talent and intelligence. This leaves to all individuals the right to occupy those situations for which their abilities best fit them." She kept her comments impersonal, so she believed, but by the time they were finished Supt. May believed himself ridiculed and offended, so that during the school term the two Hardcutt youngsters attending the high school were made to feel his rancour because of their elder sister's crusading spirit.

Miss Randall also spoke at this meeting, but on a loftier, more erudite strain than the more argumentative Miss Hardcutt. She traced the history of "the ruling woman" from tribal days down. It wasn't doubted that Miss Randall was a very educated and intellectual woman, but few people understood what she was saying and none of them understood how it could be made to apply to the cooking, mending and bringing up of children, that makes up household work.

Miss Randall was a large girl with almost awkwardly free gestures. Her carrot-coloured hair, fine, lightly freckled skin, with a blue veined tinge beneath it, and her broad generous-lipped mouth, gave her an appearance that would have been called beauty where beauty is judged less by the cornfed-health look than by distinction of appearance. Her manner to most of the townspeople and to all of her pupils was amusedly patronising. As both she and Miss Hardcutt dressed well, with clothes thought to be made in Paris, they were the objects of some attention on the part of other women in the town, but the gossips had a hard time in slaying them because of their indifference and aloofness. Some of the men whom they entertained at teas, or asked to their evenings, were deemed libertinish; Mr. Sonderland particularly. Not in the year that he'd been in town as district manager of the railroad company had he been seen with a decent woman, and he made no efforts to conceal his carryings on with waitresses about the town. However to both of these women he sent flowers, boxes of candies, came to their entertainments, and indulged in their discussions. As neither of them was ever seen alone with him, or known to have to do with him except as guest amongst other guests, a sniff was all that even Mrs. Lewis could give as insinuation when she said "For women of such reputed intelligence those two can satisfy themselves with very disreputable men. I suppose they can take care of themselves but I should not want my daughter having Mr. Sonderland as a caller, even if I stayed in the room through his call."

Miss Randall had a collection of rare edition books, some of which she leant to Miss Hardcutt, who after much persuasion in turn, allowed her young brother, Sammy, to read them. He read them insistently because Miss Randall had laughingly said he would not be able to understand them anyway. An antagonistic admiration for her existed in his young breast. He wished she'd talk straight to him instead of always seeming to laugh at and patronize him. One Sunday when his sister was feeling ill Miss Randall asked him if he didn't want to take a long walk with her, and they set off across the country and walked for four hours, from nine till one o'clock. In that time he got more acquainted with her, and instead of fearing her as too brilliant and aloof a person, he understood that her early life had been spent amongst people and in environment of much similitur to that surrounding him; and sensed her chagrin at having to return to it after life of more variety in New York City. It wasn't until ten years later however that he learned, through his sister's telling him, of the wild emotions, and the indiscreet incidents which had been a part of Miss Randall's days in the village. She stayed in town but one year however, and was gone to Chicago the next year in an attempt to become a theatrical director. An inheritance that came to her permitted her to stop teaching. However she engaged herself to be married, and had her love affair, then broke the engagement; went on to another love affair; returned for a semester's teaching in Wentworth where no one but Miss Hardcutt knew of what had happened in the interval; and very nearly became involved in a scandal because of her relationship with Jim Freeman, a young man of twenty, and six years her junior, "I wasn't made for suppression, and I couldn't tolerate marriage," she told Miss Hardcutt. "As the older men in town are impossible one must content oneself with the youngsters before they've become too awful in their small town vulgarity."

Miss Randall however left Wentworth again, and did not come back this time. As she had inherited a ranch of six thousand acres in Montana, she went there for a time, and from there went to California, and then back to New York. The last heard of her she was planning a trip to Europe, and had considerably increased her income and fortune by wise real estate speculation. By this time people had ceased to think that she was going to make a name for herself as one of the intellectual women of the country. She simply dropped out of sight and hearing of Wentworth and remained there. Of Miss Hardcutt however more was being heard; she was back in Minneapolis, was president of a woman's political league, had become a social radical, and contemplated going in for political life as a means of making a living, as school teaching had always bored her.

Both Miss Randall and Miss Hardcutt were exceptional individuals amongst the schoolteachers in town. For the main part the teachers at all the grade schools, the high school and the Normal, were either young women simply waiting for a chance to get married, frustrated unhappy little old maids, or embittered and narrow-minded ladies, or men little fitted for competency in any profession. But the spaciousness of the country and the freedom of young animal life about, permitted school children to escape the too cramping influences of petty minds if they had instincts of there being a larger-minded world outside the village.

Mrs. Alfred T. Hammer, president of the Woman's Christian Temperance Union, which was allied with the State and Inter-

State W.C.T.U., sensed in the circumstances surrounding and after the death of Mr. James an opportunity, though tactfully, for poor Mrs. James' sake, she did not want to make it too obvious that this case was to be used as an example in a Temperance drive. So she waited for over a year, and then, having heard that Mrs. James was leaving town, postponed even a few months longer, so that direct mention might be made of the case, once none of the James family were about.

Mrs. Hammer was at forty, and as a mother of four pretty children, two boys, and two girls, still a freshly pretty woman of much plump pinkness, blondness, and blue-eyed doll blankness of expression. Within some months she expected another baby, but she felt that there was time yet for her to put energy into Temperance work.

In Mrs. Hammer was little of the fanatic. She was simply a pretty woman who liked pretty clothes for herself and for her children, and she liked admiring attention. Having married as soon as she graduated from the normal school eighteen years back, she felt that she'd never been given a real opportunity to show her ability, or to reveal how intelligent and informed she was.

All her children resembled her more than they did Alfred; that is, all of them were pink and white, with yellow or light coloured hair, glass blue eyes, and innocent expressions. Either of the boys would have made pretty girls; for that matter Alfred, her husband, with his rosy cheeks, and naïve painted-wax features, would have made a pretty woman. They'd trained their children to be temperate as possible about all things. Six-year-old Harry had been promised ten dollars to put in his bank account if he'd eat no candy but milk chocolate for a year; seventeen-year-old Percy was assured of three hundred dollars on his twenty-first birthday if he could tell his father that he'd never been inside a saloon in his life and had never tasted anything alcoholic except as prescribed medicine. As things looked to Mr. and Mrs. Hammer they would have much more trouble with their daughters than with their sons. Fifteen-year-old Gladys was tractable enough, but twelve-year-old Fritzie was indisputably a tomboy, and more boisterous and impudent with grown up people than any twelve-year-old boy would have dared to be. Often she was directly disobedient to her mother.

In the past Mrs. Hammer had believed herself quite an elocutionist, so that still she took great pride in delivering speeches to members of the W.C.T.U., or upon any public occasion that gave her the opportunity. Consequently she was influential at stimulating an interest in elocution in the town, where every year contests were held amongst the Normal and High School students.

At this phase in the existence of Wentworth the small city was notable for the number of freshly beautiful young people about, many of whom showed indications of talent in some direction or other. Perhaps the climate was responsible, but particularly were there a number of girls about with amazingly fine natural singing voices, and the presence of Warren Golding made it possible for them to have their voices trained. He'd been slated for opera, but after two years of studying music in New York and abroad, he'd come back to Wentworth to live with his widowed mother who had taught history in a town school for over twenty years.

The voices seemed to run in families. All three of the Freeman girls, Gertrude, Maimie, and Katherine, possessed contralto voices of fine timbre. Both Lenore and Mabel Thompson possessed equally fine contralto voices with deeper quality of tone; and where the Freeman girls possessed only passable good looks, the Thompson girls both possessed beauty. Mabel was too calm a cameo; lazy, placid, and without temperament that showed in the way of personal magnetism, so she didn't take well when singing in public, but what she lacked in the way of vitality, sixteen year old Lenore made up for. She could have walked into any musical comedy or revue and have become a flapper star over night. Her dark red hair, and impishly piquant face, made extra nicely impudent because of a retroussé nose and forever coquetting eyes, combined with a litheness of body and grace, would have been enough in themselves had she not had a voice.

The more sensationally beautiful Helaine Blair was by now in retirement with her voice, it having been overtrained by a too enthusiastic instructor in the course of a year's study in Chicago. Her golden-eyed, flashing-rose, and luminous-white beauty, was becoming less startling too, now that the floating swanlike gesture of her carriage was being marred by her increasing plumpness. It was apparent that Lenore had by now completely outdistanced Helaine as local beauty, though her loveliness was not that of perfect facial features. She had wit, audacity, almost insolence of bearing, but she thought more quickly than Helaine ever had, or than any of the older generation who'd made dignity and grace their fetish. Lenore was the new tradition. She swore richly, when she was angry, which was frequently. She told her parents where to get off at if they tried to stop her in her enjoyments; she smoked cigarettes when sitting in an automobile with young admirers— when ladies were not smoking cigarettes; and at sixteen she was going for automobile drives and staying out all hours of the night, without being talked about as fast. People simply deemed Lenore a spoiled, self-willed, and disrespectful little girl, trying to act grown up, and trying to imitate the noisy Mrs. Allen. By the time Lenore came into the scene in Wentworth the Fitzgerald girls, Mary Warden, and the two older Freeman girls were all looked upon as middle aged, though none of them had more than passed twenty-five. It had become in a five year period well nigh impossible for any girl who desired to be known as a classy dresser to be seen more than twice in the same ball dress. The farm community about Wentworth was a prosperous one; eggs, potatoes, and other produce were by now being shipped to the cities in great quantities; cattle, hogs, horses, poultry, and all the grains were being raised on thousands of fertile acres surrounding the town. A revised idea of what wealth meant had already begun to unseat families formerly mighty.

Not only were new families that came into the town unseating former potentates, and belles, but also once pitied and despised families were becoming people who needed to be noticed. Few of the girls of the twenty to thirty-year-old generation had managed to marry; some of them finally married men they'd once scoffed at. After a trip abroad Mary Warden taught school for several years, and then married the owner of a barber shop; soon after her marriage Dolly Fitzgerald married a man working in the barber shop, though she managed to get him finally into her father's hardware store. Gertrude Freeman, people suspected, would have been glad of the chance to marry Isaac Stein, the Jewish haberdashery store owner. Other girls married travelling salesmen, and store clerks. But most of them did not marry. They taught school, an occupation that gave them little opportunity to meet men.

Mrs. Hammer, observing, or rather feeling, all that was happening about her, felt that her daughters needed to be taught to face events with less open exuberance and extravagance of pace when young. She'd been murmuring at club meetings about culture and refinement for some time; her children were all taking music lessons, violin or piano, and she encouraged them to read literature, as she knew it. The restlessness of vitality, the malcontent, that possessed so many of the young people in town, but that had no direction, she was sure needed directing.

So Mrs. Hammer suggested to the W.C.T.U. members that they offer prizes to be given at an elocution contest in which the subjects elocuted upon would all be taken from the Temperance viewpoint. The date of the contest was fixed for six weeks ahead, and its taking place was announced in the weekly paper. At first there was little interest shown by the young people in town until it was realized that the first prize was to be two hundred dollars; the second one hundred and fifty; the third one hundred; with three other prizes of fifty dollars each. Upon this realization the Public Library was besieged for books containing possible recitations, and Mrs. Jones found herself called upon to lend her own, and to discover other books of prose and poetical pieces dealing with prohibition.

Not a young man, or boy, however, entered the contest; most of them giggled and burlesqued Ten Nights in the Barroom, or recited grave and ludicrous tales on the horrors of drink. However an undercurrent of doubt ran beneath all of their fooling. There began now to be about some horrible tales of the consequences of drink, and Mr. James was recalled. Old Ike Sorenson too was remembered. All in all it appeared that the examples of the horrors consequent upon intemperance were frequent, though few cases of a fury of craving for drink such as blasted the lives and homes told of in pieces to be recited at the contest were known. That an original incompetence of life, and a devastating sense of its futility, rather than an inherent yearning for drink might have been the cause of Mr. James's drinking, and for his disruption, did not occur to the minds of beings possessed of so much animal vitality of life as most of those living in Wentworth.

The night of the contest arrived, and there were twelve contestants for the six prizes to be given. Among them were Katherine Freeman, Lenore Thompson, Gladys Hammer, and a girl from out of town who attended the Normal School, Elsie Linquist. She was an ungainly girl of sixteen, with an intelligent-eyed face, abrupt gestures, and an overgrown body which had come upon her so quickly that she did not know how yet to control its actions well.

Amongst the other competitors there was too, seventeen-year-old Olive La Brec. Mrs. Hammer had been reluctant that she should enter the competition, because it seemed hardly right that a La Brec girl should be permitted to compete for a prize with her own daughter, Gladys. However there had been no way to prevent that entry.

Several of the contestants recited and were duly applauded; and then a ripple went through the audience as it was announced that Lenore Thompson would be the next on the program. All of the young men in town sat up. It was generally conceded amongst them that Lenore was some kid, and that for all her pep and recklessness you couldn't get gay with her without getting a bang on the ear that let you know Lenore was no feeble dame.

Lenore came upon the stage, and the audience sat up to take notice of her. It was needed. To celebrate the occasion she had had her black-red hair bobbed, a thing unknown for any girl beyond

61

childhood years. It curled cutely around her jaunty head. On the side of her right eye she had pasted a star of black court plaster. Her few freckles were not noticeable in the stagelight; she was wearing a white lace dress that clung to her slight figure as though it liked her. There was not about her manner, as there had been about that of all the girls who had preceded her, a trace of stagefright. She stepped to the center of the stage, announced the title of her selection, and began with young deliberation. All of the speakers before her had chosen tales of individual and family lives blasted and degraded through drink; Lenore, however, on the advice of Miss Randall, a teacher new to the town this year and recently graduated from Columbia University, had chosen to narrate statistics and the findings of a research, aided by Miss Randall, on the consequences of drink in small towns. Nevertheless her address held the attention of the audience more than had that of any of the girls who had preceded, and great applause, whistling, stamping of feet, and insistence that she return for three bows, followed. Much of that applause naturally was from her boy admirers.

Gladys Hammer came on next. Her mother felt a pang of jealousy because her reception was in nowise so enthusiastic as that accorded Lenore, but she solaced herself with the thought that her daughter was more ladylike. Standing, poised in her delivery too, Gladys was as daintily pretty in the foam of pink dress that clad her as a spray of cherry blossoms could be. She too had chosen a not too melodramatic theme, and held the audience easily. Mrs. Hammer could not know after Gladys had finished how to judge what the judges would decide though she was sure that her girl's recitation was much less pretentious. The applause for Gladys was enthusiastic too, and came, Mrs. Hammer hoped, from the older members of the audience rather than girl-mad boys.

Two more contestants rendered their recitations, and it was apparent the audience were getting restive. Mrs. Hammer felt she should have held Gladys and Lenore till the last as everybody would surely have waited to hear them. Of course there was

Katherine Freeman to come, but she wasn't much interested in her subject, and was too often heard singing in public to have a very fresh interest. The evening was over certainly—

Until Elsie Linquist, the out-of-town girl, came upon the stage. She came on rather awkwardly and her dress was a plain dark blue one. There was an appeal in her clumsiness however, the beauty of raw youngness. Her voice as she started speaking was husky and deep; it remained so, and gathered power. There was force in her gestures, and in the variations of tone in her voice. Mrs. Hammer was not sure that she wasn't among the real competitors for the first prize.

At last all of the contestants had spoken but Olive La Brec, and Mrs. Hammer settled into her seat with a satisfied feeling that all was over and the judges might as well retire, though of course the form of hearing the La Brec girl had to be gone through. Mrs. Hammer could not recall which one of the La Brecs this one was, there were so many of them, all tow or red-headed, freckled, and shanty Irish in their quality.

When Olive La Brec came on people began to register surprise. It was known that by now she had three sisters who were grown up, and making money somewhere, as stenographers—one was in the millinery business—but where had she got a dress like that? It was distinctly the most expensive dress worn that evening, and of the latest mode that nobody had thought of daring to wear in Went-worth, though cut, bobbied effect, the thick cloth of green olive with rusted gold designs about it clinging to her slender limbs. Of course that older sister of hers who was secretary to an attorney in Minneapolis had given it to her; and she also had shown Olive how to do up her gleaming orange hair. It was shameful for a seventeen-year-old girl to look like some visiting concert singer for all the impression she created on the stage. And the dress revealed her body so sensuously.

Olive had chosen to give a humourous sketch, and prefixed it with the explanation, "I thought that most of the selections would be extremely serious tonight, so I chose one for myself that might be amusing without slighting the theme that we all have to speak upon."

A great deal of laughter and hilarity was caused by her characterized delivery. After she left the stage there was as much applause and shouting, so far as could be judged, as there had been for Lenore Thompson.

Five minutes later Attorney Scott was on the platform, announcing the decision. He spoke:

"It has been difficult for us all to make decisions confronted with so much beauty and talent as we have been this evening. We should like to give every contestant the first prize. However—the first prize goes to—a—yes, Miss Linquist, who is a stranger amongst us I believe. It was deemed that for dramatic effectiveness, and for presentation of the theme as specified by the rules of the contest, Miss Linquist had displayed the clearest understanding, and greatest variety of dramatic talent."

"The second prize we have had some difficulty with, and would almost like to ask that it go both to Miss Thompson and Miss La Brec, for originality of choice, and for considered presentation. However as that is not possible we have solved the issue by announcing our decision of a tie so far as our appreciations are concerned, and by granting the second prize to Miss Thompson, as it is understood that her recitation was of her own composition. Naturally the third prize goes to Miss La Brec. While the three remaining prizes go to Miss Hammer, Miss Freeman, and Miss Amberson."

Mrs. Hammer, who expected her baby to arrive within two months time, found herself unable at the moment to put further effort into W.C.T.U. work. She couldn't righteously argue that the award of the prizes was unfair; she could for Gladys think so however. How different Wentworth had become without her having been aware of the change that was taking place within it. There always had been the Normal School with the influx of new girls it brought to town every year, but now there were new families resident in town, so that it was hard keeping in touch with the histories of them all.

The Reeves family, the old people anyway, were certainly having bad luck piled up on them. Until two years ago both of them had always been generous and goodnatured. Old man Reeves never took advantage of his wealth, or of his position as President of the First National Bank, to best anybody in a business deal.

His bad luck started with the marriage of his oldest daughter, Irene, to a mere tailor's clerk. For two years she'd been away at a private girls school in Washington, and though deemed ugly, came back to Wentworth dashingly stylish, arrogant, and contemptuous. But she had some right to be indifferent to town girls as none of them had ever been decently friendly to her. School days over, it was thought she'd take to travelling, or living in some city as had the unmarried Warden and Fitzgerald girls, but instead she suddenly eloped with a tailor, and it looked as if the support of her and her husband would rest on old man Reeves.

Then Peter Reeves, as soon as he reached fifteen, changed from a shy, dull-mannered boy, into a reckless boy about town. His sandy coloured head could be seen all around the country as he sped about in the family car breaking all speed limits. And there was always some girl of not a very good class with him. One day he collided with another car, and he and the driver of the other car, a man from out of town, were both killed. It was little wonder that old man Reeves and his wife were both aging so much in this last year as it was well known too that a lot of money had been lost in the bank through a bad investment made by old man Reeves' younger partner.

The silly, ugly Dolly Reeves too, had begun to play around with travelling salesmen, and she wasn't discreet about the way she did it; moreover by this time enough young people of Wentworth had been away at private schools, or at college, and enough of an attitude about what is not done had developed, so that girls of good families had to be rather careful about how they met the trains. It wasn't the reputation of fastness they gained; it was simply the reputation of being such deadheads that they were driven to that for pastime, that girls didn't want now.

When Old Man Reeves moved out of town, it looked about time, if he was going to save any face for himself at all. Little news drifted back about the family, except that it was understood that Don Reeves, who'd been Glenn Warden's chum while they were at high school, had married a wealthy girl in the East. When it was heard two years later that he was making quite a success as an attorney there was little doubt that it was his wife's money that had done it.

Mrs. Kinney skimmed through the pages of the *Ladies' Farm Journal* feeling a martyr to duty and to her own courageous sense of the fatality of things. Times were so hard; she was so ailing, with kidney trouble, backaches, headaches, neuralgia, nervous prostration, and female troubles but little understood. She glimpsed enough of the article on raising chickens that were egg layers to conclude that she must at some less tired moment read it; she might even go into the chicken raising business to help family expenses; or she might try bees as a later article in the journal suggested. It sounded simple to make money off bees or chickens in these articles, if one only exercised a little care. If Mr. Kinney weren't so shiftless, and if the children would only try to help her, their poor overworked mother, a little, instead of them all letting her break her back attending to their needs!

Soon Mrs. Kinney was at the back pages of the journal where the advertisements were. Then her interest began to pick up. Here was a small advertisement, suggesting a way for girls and boys to make money. She would clip that and give it to Lizzie. It probably was only another one of those companies that wanted children to sell perfumes, or subscriptions for them, and gave the children in return some cheap jewelry, but even so Lizzie would like it. She

knew by now that it never came to anything if after getting the
jewelry, and perfumes, or subscription blanks, if it was a publication, she did nothing further. Of course there were always threat-
ening letters.

And surely, Mrs. Kinney reflected, she must send in to see what
this new medicine for kidney trouble was. The idea of pills to be
taken in sequence sounded right sensible to her. And perhaps the
capsules to be used twice a week would be more effective than the
ones she was trying now. Of course the seat of all her trouble was
female ailment.

Mr. Kinney, veterinarian, came into the dining room to sit by
the table that was by now cleared of the supper dishes. The light
was clearer here, and besides there was Mrs. Kinney to talk to, and
he felt conversational, if mildly impatient with his sighing wife,
Annie. She was leaning over her farm paper, as usual he supposed,
reading patent medicine advertisements.

"It seems to me Annie, if instead of complaining about how
little we have to live on you'd save some of the money you spend
on patent medicine, we would get on. But I suppose there's no use
talking to you of that. You will keep all the cupboards and bureaus
messed up with your pills and bottles."

"Well now Henry, you haven't six children around you in the
house all the time, with everlasting headaches a driving you wild.
And you know you don't want there to be any more young ones
any more than I do with the trouble we have getting on now.

Mr. Kinney settled his aging figure into an easy chair, and
grunted a reply. His sporting vest was spotted, and his trousers
bagged at the knees. Not for the last five years had he looked dapper
and stylish as once he did in the days when he was more of a
sporting man.

"Gracie ought to be coming to see us tonight," Mrs. Kinney
spoke, and sighed in reflection again, thinking of the month-ago
elopement of her nineteen-year-old daughter with a clerk at the
Amberson shoestore.

"O Grace is too much taken up with her young man yet to be

counted on for paying any attention to the parents that reared her," Mr. Kinney grunted, by now well into a detective story he'd started. "I never can get that girl. She was one of the best-looking girls around town, and clever enough too. Well, she's made her bed. Let her sleep in it. If I could I wouldn't put myself out to help support that husband of hers."

Mrs. Kinney sniffed and made no reply. Mr. Kinney, feeling the atmosphere heavy, moved, having decided to go down town. He'd see if some of the boys at the livery stable wouldn't want a game of poker over at the Commercial Hotel; or there might be some travelling salesmen around the hotel who made the town regularly and were old cronies of his. Mrs. Kinney didn't object to his going as she had in her mind an intention to answer several of the advertisements for medicine, and for making money in the home, that she'd marked in various magazines. Her husband wouldn't scold her, but she felt ill at ease writing these letters when he was around, because he would ask her who she was writing to, and would guess, and make her feel his disapproval which he held in reserve. Female ailments aren't a husband's or a man's province anyway.

But Mrs. Kinney didn't write her letters either; she felt too tired she decided, and thought she'd go over to call on Mrs. Spear about the family washing. Mrs. Spear knew she was to come for the wash on Thursday, but Mrs. Kinney rather wanted to talk to her. She wanted to hear the end of that story about Mrs. Allen and her trouble with her husband over a lover. Mrs. Spear was always well posted about what was going on in town, and even if she was a washerwoman, she was right interesting to talk to; a real lively woman if her husband had only let her alone so there weren't so many young ones around the house.

The Grand Theatre, seldom open for the summer months, was open now, and to the biggest public that ever entered its doors, through the longest period of time.

For almost a week everybody in town had wondered who Mr.

Goyer was, and what occupied his attention in Wentworth. His thin, muscular body, a face with a seemingly bored expression, had a veiled hawklike keenness. His shiny black hair was always in order, as was a well-waxed, pointed mustache. It was judged from his tailorishly groomed appearance that he must be connected with the stage; an advance press agent of a circus perhaps. Then advertisements announcing a loom-end sale began to appear on all billboards about the town and country. Boys were hired to carry signs through the streets, and any youngster could be fairly sure of a half day's work by applying to Mr. Goyer who would give him handbills to distribute at doorsteps through Wentworth and its suburbs.

For three nights before the official opening of the loom-end sale a free show was put on at the theatre. The whole town was agog. A travelling hypnotist was appearing; he was a magician as well, and with him was a male comedian and a girl singer of racy songs. Besides these out of town entertainers, Miss Anderson, elocution teacher at the Normal School, was to recite comic and dramatic pieces, while Maimie Freeman, and Mabel Thompson were each to sing a solo. The hypnotist, also a mind reader, would send his assistant through the audience, and he from the stage would answer questions written on paper handed to the assistant by members of the audience.

The first night—the theatre was packed—there was some trouble because town rowdies hooted and catcalled from the galleries too much, as Bull Norton was drunk himself, and was passing around the whiskey to the others. As they became intoxicated, they called out vulgar and profane remarks to the entertainers on the stage, particularly to the girl singer of racy songs.

"Meet me in the alley after the show, kiddo," Gus Johnson, mild when sober, shouted out, aided in his recklessness by a pint of whiskey in him. The singer was whining out,

Come all ye belly shakers,
come all ye baby makers,
come, come, all, to the hootchy kootchy show,

and by singing this song caused herself to be stopped by Mr. Goyer. Clearly, he realized he should have been more careful about selecting a professional lady entertainer in a town with so many churches as Wentworth had. Not only the girl singer, but the male comedian, and the hypnotist made several cracks that went down well enough with the toughs in the gallery, but Mr. Goyer didn't expect them to buy much loom-end goods from him.

The first day of the sale came on. As early as seven o'clock a throng of women from the country and the outskirts of town were already assembled in front of the doors of the theatre to have first pick of the goods displayed. Courtesy was abandoned for this day, as they jostled and argued with each other to have places nearest the door.

"I hear he's bought out three bankrupt stores," Mrs. Ike Samuelson declared.

"Bosh," said Mrs. Lewis, whose face was gleaming with decision not to be shoved out of her place by any farm wife, "he's done nothing but collect all the unsaleable goods from wholesale houses in the city. You can depend upon it, there isn't more than enough goods in his whole collection than will serve as bait. I intend looking very closely at what I purchase, and will buy nothing that I don't recognize as bait material. I shan't get into the hysteria of buying simply because of faked bargains."

It was ten o'clock before the doors of the theatre were opened, and by this time a virtual stampede was on amongst the town and farm ladies assembled. The best center smash football squad in ten states could not have plowed through the jam. Where few courtesies were exchanged by the mob at seven, nothing but argumentation, and accusation, and elbowing took place now. With the opening of the doors there was a mob rush, smash, squash, and bang through the portals, which did not subside for five minutes. By that time women were scurrying up and down the aisles of counters where goods were placed. Shoes for the baby; underwear for the entire family; stockings; wash and woolen goods; small pieces of cloth that would do for crazy quilting if for nothing else;

hats, gloves, table linen and towelling; and other materials, were purchased recklessly by women sure that they had a bargain, and suspicious of all other women about, who stood as if they were going to take the very bargains out of each other's hands. Within two hours however the first enthusiastic zeal had calmed down; and the loom-end sale settled into a three days' run of grim persistency.

Ladies retired from the sale at twelve to serve quickly prepared lunches to their families; they were back by one thirty, and bought till six. In the evening they examined their goods, and were sure they'd been taken in. Deciding that they would not attend the sales on the morrow, they retired, fatigued, to be again at the theatre the next day at an early hour.

Mrs. Lewis told Mrs. Hardcutt three days after the sale that she had never been inveigled into buying so much trash in her life before. Such a man as Mr. Goyer had not ought to be allowed in town. But he was back next year, and made more money the second year than he had the first, because after much discussion it was decided amongst the ladies that by purchasing enough one might get something worth while for a half, or even a third price, and that was an allurement, even if all other goods purchased had to be discarded or given to paupers.

It having been demonstrated by Mr. Goyer how capacious the Grand Theatre was when empty of its seats, Mrs Lewis at once began to propagande for giving the Annual Foreign Mission dinner there this year, and had it suggested at the various churches from the pulpit, except of course that the Catholics never had anything to do with these movements upon the part of the Baptists, Methodists, Unitarians, and Presbyterians, all of which churches were on amiable footings with each other in their need to stand united against Catholicism.

Into Mrs. Lewis' fading, but still observant, and sharply-piercing eye came a new glisten. Her matronly figure could be seen going about making calls upon various ladies whom she believed lax in their efforts to aid this dinner, and in the gait of her walk was purpose. At the houses of all Presbyterian ladies she made a few comments on the Rev. Robinson, though she was not so indiscreet as to let ladies of other congregations realize that the congregation—namely Deacon Pothatch and herself—of the Presbyterian Church were not yet, after seven experiments, satisfied that it had procured a minister to its liking.

"It seems impossible in this generation to get a man who is orthodox, and who realizes the reverence of his calling. Not that I deny Rev. Robinson's mental capacity—his sermons are well delivered; but they have no fervour. And that he should play tennis, and be so easily accessible as a companion to men such as—need I mention names—ah—."

"But Mrs. Lewis," Mrs. Hammer, a woman with the public interest at heart herself but intending to be just, discussed with Mrs. Lewis, "The Reverend is hardly friendly to Mr. Jenkins. It is only at tennis that the two meet, and then through Mr. Scott mainly. I think we could permit the minister that game—"

"Indeed—I believe it as meretricious as the horse-racing of Rev. Jameson, who, though he shows doubtful taste in setting up in the piano business in the very town where he was minister, was simple enough a man to be forgiven because one realizes the coarse stock he must have come from. But the Rev. Robinson is a man supposedly of culture, with a sense of propriety—"

But Mrs. Lewis would recall that she had more calls to make, and would depart from whichever lady she was discussing the Rev. Robinson with, and she would feel within herself that at least her duty had been done in the way of honest expression, and that she was no woman to rest once she had a disagreeable duty to carry through to the disagreeable end.

At nine o'clock on the morning the Missions dinner was to be given, Percy Jones and Carl Toppen started out in Deacon Pothatch's wagon to collect the provisions which various women about town were to give to be served at the dinner and supper. Mrs. Lewis had carefully prepared a routed list for them. Mrs. Scott had promised three loaves of pressed meat; Mrs. Hardcutt was to give two chocolate cakes; Mrs. Anderson, two crocksfull of potato salad; Mrs. Amberson baked beans; others gave apple, pumpkin, raisin, or mince meat pies, cold roast chicken; roast beef, veal, etc. The bakery was furnishing the bread; the Harms Grocery Stores furnished the coffee; the ice cream parlours the ice cream; and so on through a long list. By twelve o'clock the boys had their wagon full, and drove back to the theatre to unload so that some of this could be served with food brought by various ladies in person to the theatre. Then they were served their meal, hovering of course about the serving tables to see that they got the best food, which they knew, as rumour and testing of the various ladies' cooking had taught them what ladies in town were to be esteemed for food preparation. After an hour they sallied forth, bloated and cheerful, to complete the collection of provisions that would be served at the evening meal. Mrs. Lewis, generally austere and forbidding, they had thought, was most gracious to them, as they had been so helpful at getting the food set upon a supply table where she could survey it. Not so much by common consent amongst the other ladies helping to serve the townspeople, as by superior aggressiveness on the part of Mrs. Lewis, was she managing the routine of service. There were a few uncomfortable moments when Mrs. Lewis' authority was questioned, but her consciousness of her executive ability saved her from being unkindly irritated by them. As when Mrs. Hardcutt suggested to Mrs. Lewis that if she'd simply wait on the table assigned to her, or portion out food to others who would wait upon it, instead of trying to direct other women who were not her servants, things would go on smoothly enough.

But it was a very successful day; and it was agreed by various women that more lawn socials would have to be given in the future because the men folk really had learned that to patronize dinners and luncheons given by ladies' organizations in this town meant a distinctly good meal. The Methodist ladies particularly knew that they had amongst their ranks cooks who could compete with the finest chefs in the country.

Leaving the theatre at nine o'clock in the evening, after all meals had been served and the theatre's interior was entirely after-a-banquet in appearance, Mrs. Hardcutt commented to Mrs. Scott, that though she'd been bad enough this year, somehow Mrs. Lewis wasn't so insistently bossy as in former years.

"It's her husband," Mrs. Scott responded crisply, "and her daughter. Haven't you heard? That young attorney in the city jilted her daughter. And of course we all know what Mr. Lewis' frequent trips to the city mean. And now he is—at fifty-five years of age, think of it—letting himself be seen about with waitresses from the Commercial House."

Mrs. Deacon Pothatch, who was trailing behind the other two ladies heard this remark. Hum—she mused to herself—it was about time that Mrs. Lewis had something to keep her in her place. But Mrs. Deacon Pothatch wouldn't have ventured to remark this; her husband and Mrs. Lewis were always in accord about the necessity of ridding their church of its present minister and trying a new one who had more orthodox ideas. They might clash on some points—and indeed they had clashed on the matter of extending cordial invitations to all people, converted by Dr. Miller's evangelism, to join the First Presbyterian Church. Mrs. Lewis had then declared in no unsure tones that there would be no backsliding riff-raff in the church if she could prevent it.

But Mrs. Pothatch wouldn't be one to oppose Mrs. Lewis. She was not a forceful person. Meekly she went, but she did doubt—she did—but of course, people are as they are, and she supposed she'd have to put up with them, whoever they were.

Mrs. Allen, Freda, was a large woman with henna coloured hair, dyed undoubtedly. Large cold blue eyes, a prominent nose, and a sensuous but generous mouth, were her other features. Her husband had a bright yellow colour scheme also but his joviality was less noisy, and more insinuating, though his flirtations with women who came into his drygoods store, and his paternal chucking of pretty girls under the chin, might pass as business suavity. It was difficult to understand how he let his wife go on. She was all over town in the automobile so that he would seldom have had a chance to use it had he wished. Surely he didn't think that so flamboyant a woman as his wife was innocent in her relationship with Dr. Boyd, the dentist, who was known as the lover of married women. She and Dr. Boyd could be seen all about the town and country almost any time of the day, and it seemed as though her boisterous laughter could be heard in any part of town wherever she was.

Dr. Boyd was supposed to have been the lover of Mrs. Todd too, whose husband, a travelling salesman, was gone for two and three week periods from town. She was flashy also, though not so flagrant as Mrs. Allen; and she, like Mrs. Allen, made no effort to acquaint herself with Wentworth society life. Except for a few bridge playing people she knew nobody; and nobody knew much of her activities except that she came and went from town a good deal.

Dr. Boyd was a complete rake and bounder; he'd never pay any attention to marriageable girls; certainly he hadn't enough clients to support himself by dentistry. But Mr. Allen seemed not at all to object to his attentions to Mrs. Allen. He'd even been known to ask Dr. Boyd what Freda intended to do "this evening"; a strange situation when a husband has to ask another man about his own wife's plans.

One day in the middle of summer Mrs. Allen came into the Bargain Dept. Store, where she seldom appeared. "Where is my husband?" she demanded of Myrtle Nelson, a clerk. Soon Mr. Allen showed up.

"I want money—five hundred dollars. I'm going to the city— and tonight," Freda Allen said. Her face was flushed, and her manner intense. "I'm through with this damned town; I'm through with you and your cheap bargain store. I'm done. Damn you and all the rest of it."

"Not so loud, not so loud," Mr. Allen cautioned her, looking

75

furtively around to see if any of his customers could hear what she was saying. "What's brought this on so suddenly? You were all right this morning."

"Tommy (Dr. Boyd) is not coming back to town. The caddish scoundrel. He might have said something to me and faced the music. See, this telegram. He's married to some girl in Iowa and is going to settle in the town the girl lives in. I knew he had some trick on his mind."

"But Freda, he's nothing to you—"

"Christ, don't make me strike you. Don't act the innocent to me. Did you ever think I was so blind I didn't know you were playing around with fool girls? You didn't think I gave a damn, or wasn't able to play my own game too, did you? But I'm going to the city now, unless you want something worse to happen. And you're going to give me money to go there and live."

"Wait Freda, we'll have to talk this over; I really can't afford five hundred at this time—anyway, how will the city solve this?" Mr. Allen said. Freda, looking at him, saw the real indifference in his expression.

"Good God" she said hysterically, "you complacent, oily lizard. A floorwalker, my husband,—O let me get out of here. But listen—you may regret not giving me the money. It might be bad advertising for your business that you didn't."

The next week's paper discreetly announced the death of Mrs. Allen, suggesting that by accident she had taken poison from a bottle she'd believed to contain a tonic. This discretion on the part of the editor deceived no one however, as hearers of her last conversation with her husband had rapidly spread that. The suicide wasn't such a surprise to the town as that of Mrs. Jenkins had been though, because it had always been apparent that the Allens meant nothing to each other, and Freda had never disguised her infatuation for Dr. Boyd.

Mr. Allen showed few signs of being affected; he remained brickish of complexion and healthy looking; ready to bandy with women customers who came into his store. People wondered if after a time he wouldn't try perhaps to marry Rhoda Blair, the beautiful Helaine's sister, who had worked in his store for years. He did not however; within a year he'd sold his store and left town to locate somewhere in the State of Oregon.

It was scarcely respectable of Mrs. Spear, the way she had a baby every year—oftener than every year. Already at thirty five she was the mother of fifteen, four of them two pairs of twins.

Mr. Spear too was a horrible example. His family, which lived in a town some hundred miles from Wentworth, was a small village family of good breeding and standing in the community. His sisters were school teachers; one brother was the mayor of the village he lived in, and his mother was a woman of refinement from a good New England family. But here was he, Fred Spear, letting his wife take in washings now and then to help keep the family going.

Mrs. Spear however seemed not to feel this greatly. She liked to complain about the hardness of life, as a bit of social conversation. With other women she'd exchange ideas on the hardness of a woman's and a mother's lot, but a listener might sense complacency in her remarks, as though she felt herself identified and made important through being a specially selected victim of fate's hardness. She'd only been a farmer's hired girl when Fred married her, and his family thought they could he suppose to her, well, they could see that this wonderful son of theirs—and them so elegant—wasn't able to take care of his family alone.

Her wiry body, clad in a loose-fitting and much stained wrapper, would stand before the washtub. Occasionally she would lean over and apathetically rub some piece of clothing on the washboard in an indifferent attempt to clean it. But soon she would straighten herself into the sagging erectness customary to her, and go on with conversation, extracting information on various townspeople from whatever neighbor or wash client or son or daughter happened to be her audience. Or she might be giving information.

Billy Hardcutt found it difficult to keep away from Mrs. Spear's place on the ragged edges of town. There were so many children around there to play with, all from five to ten years old, near his own seven. And Mrs. Spear never stopped him or them from making mud pies. And the swamp lay in that direction too so that if he and other youngsters wanted to go frogging, or hunting birds' eggs in the woods beyond, Mrs. Spear's place was a good starting point. He began coming one day when his mother sent him there to find out about the washing. Unclean a washerwoman as she was, she had to be used sometimes because Mrs. O'Reilly was forever giving up washing and going in for cooking, and Mrs. Spear at least returned all pieces, which the Ford and Higgins women were not so apt to do.

"Billy Hardcutt, you'll have to quit running over to those awful Spears and letting that scandal-monging hag bleed you of all our private family information," Agnes Hardcutt told Billy frequently. "You tell her all you know of everybody in town, and then some. You're a worse gossip than she is with your tittle tattle."

At these moments Billy had to sneak out into the back yard to be away from scolding, and to wonder what he'd told Mrs. Spear now. It wasn't his fault, he brooded. Why were there so many things a person couldn't talk about, and why did family things have to always be secret? Mrs. Spear would give him bread and syrup with her own children, and then begin talking about people, and of course he had to answer questions—and where else in town were there as many pets to play with? All the stray dogs about usually landed there for a few days' stay, and Billy's mother wouldn't have a dog about the place. He always knew that if he got hold of a guinea pig, a kitten, or even a young pelican, Mrs. Spear would manage to have one of her children find a place to keep it until it died, or you had to get rid of it because it was so covered with lice. And besides Billy could learn things at the Spears' when nobody else would answer his questions, but he knew he couldn't explain that to his mother. If she ever caught him jacking-off a dog the way Rog

Spear had taught him he'd get the hide tanned off him, but it was too funny, seeing the expression on the dog's face.

Mr. Spear, a well built man of some six feet two inches, and a good natured rough-going temperament, was sheriff of the county, but that position paid little, and what little it paid he spent elsewhere than on his family mainly, as he rarely stayed at home. There were too many children to occupy the beds and eat the food. He must however have stayed home one night or so a year for every year brought a new offspring, and Mrs. Spear's marital chastity was not questioned in the community. Unlike Mrs. Deb Bonner, it had never been thought of her by young men about town that her large family indicated that she was loose in her morals. But Mrs. Bonner had only seven children, and was still passably good looking, and only twenty eight years old. Mrs. Spear never could have been much to make a young man randy.

The only mystery about the Spear family was how they managed not to be considered paupers and white trash as were the Ford and Higgins outfits, members of which families were always more employed and earned far more money than the Spears. But even Mrs. Lewis would have been willing to ask Mrs. Spear to wait on table at a Missions dinner, if work were heavy. That never could have happened to a Ford or Higgins. The whole subtle line and romance of class distinction might be traced in the attitudes that townspeople had towards these families, all of which were equally, in being, complete ly, incompetent beyond the boundaries of existence, and none of the members of which were possessed of any passion of revolt against whatever might occur in fate's calendar.

Twenty years in Wentworth had not served to make old Mrs. McPherson intimate with anybody in town; even with her step-son-in-law's wife and family. Her husband, a furniture dealer, had considerable money; she had more. They lived alone in a big white house on the corner of Egan Avenue and 5th Street. Its great lawn, always well kept, had been a life saver for five generations of boys needing pocket money. In the summer the mowing of it, and in the winter the cutting of wood for Mrs. McPherson, was the first thought of a boy who wanted to earn spending money.

Her beautiful all-white hair had just a slightly lemon tinge through it on the top of the head; elsewhere it was glistening white. Her blue eyes were keen, and her manner cryptic, though not unkind, but her grandsons, Bobbie and Dutch, never felt towards her as though she were a grandma, as they did towards Grandma Amberson.

She was simply a figure meant for a more cosmopolitan life, but the village encompassed her. She could have no interest in the social life amongst the class of people who surrounded her, in the beginning, so that the few beings who gradually came to live in town who might have formed a nucleus for a fairly gracious society, came too late for her to change her habit of life, that of expecting nothing outside herself and accepting a routine guided by herself. Only to the very young generation of boys, from eight to sixteen, did she go with interest, and then only if they struck her as extraordinarily alert. Often she would call one of the Hardcutt, or Reynalds boys to her, and ask him if he didn't want a job, cleaning windows, chopping wood, or mowing the lawn. She would be strict with him however if he didn't do his job well; he could take his time, but he had to do his work carefully.

She puzzled Sammy Hardcutt, who worked for her more than any other boy did at this period. She didn't give him advice, and never asked questions—as though she had no curiosity. Maybe she didn't need to be talking to prove things to herself; or perhaps when a person gets so old as she was—seventy—wonder stops the questions and the curiosity.

Wentworth was coming on; by now several young men and women of the town were college people, yet in college, or graduated. Gene Collins, after two years at the State University was appointed to

West Point, and his first year there made a great name for himself as a football player. By this time any friendship that had existed between him and Peter Reynalds had evaporated. Six years had passed. Peter, who had moved four years before to Chicago, found upon revisiting Wentworth that they were completely antipathetic to each other. Gene's attitude about money, a tightfisted one, was the first symptom; and his intentness on making a good marriage was a second. But most of all was Peter's inability to be interested in Gene's athletic career, or to care for him whether he made good at West Point or not. It seemed to him so ridiculous a gesture on Gene's part, if he had any talent or unusual intelligence that he should be willing to harness it to a thing such as military discipline, which would effectively crush all his inventiveness; and Gene never would be a man of strategic genius.

Even roadshows, of plays that had been hits in New York not more than six years back, were beginning to be sent to Wentworth; the third or fourth companies naturally. And two farmers had been known to build houses on their farms with modern improvements—bathtubs on a farm in a community where fifteen years back a bathtub was scarcely known in the wealthiest village home.

Book Two

For three days an intense heat dominated all life and movement throughout the area of Wentworth. The thoroughfares were covered with dust a foot deep, so that vehicles passing through them left immense clouds of dust which made the atmosphere deadly choking for minutes afterwards.

Old Ike Sorenson, after a week's dutiful attendance to his crops, had come into town on this day, already drunk from liquor he had at his bachelor shack ten miles from town. It was a drink he called mithigulum, a preparation made of yeast, honey and water, which he let stand supposedly ten days after making. Ike however frequently let this preparation stand thirty days, as he always had several crocksful on hand, and by this time it had become firefully potent; this and corn silage whiskey drained from the bottom of his cylindrical silo where the juices of the winter ago silage had seeped, served him when he didn't feel up to a trip to town for a drink.

For the first hour Ike wandered up and down the street, with red restless gaze, and a staggering indifference to all kidding comments or looks of disapproval. His dirty sandy beard was unkempt as was his sand coloured mop of hair. His bleary blue eyes were besottedly sullen and feverish with an animal sullenness.

"Ay tank you giff me more vhiskey," he asked of Jake Murphy at Sullivan's saloon, but Jake was reluctant to take his order because Ike was sometimes dangerous when he got drunk, and wanted to fight every man he saw. Women he ignored. The saloons in the town and county were having enough trouble fighting the prohibition movement without serving Ike, who wasn't good enough a customer with his periodic drunk-ons, on cheap liquor, to make it worth while pampering him.

But Ike got strong liquor somewhere; possibly from old man Higgins who at the moment appeared flush with money so that it was supposed he was running a blind pig at his shack, in conjunction with a brothel in which his own daughters were the inmates who served the farmhands and hoboes that patronized the place. At any rate it was sure that he dealt in bootleg liquor, so that failing elsewhere, Ike naturally went to him.

Ike, being thoroughly drunk by twelve o'clock, staggered along Egan Avenue until he got to Mrs. Simpson's tiny house next to the Masonic Lodge. He was sure that she wouldn't kick him out even if she discovered him sleeping under her sacks of coal in the woodshed back of her kitchen.

Mrs. Simpson, Brick's mother, was a woman nearly fifty, of German stock. She said, in her more lucid moments, that her husband, a very wealthy man, had deserted her when they arrived in America, but nobody really believed she'd ever had a husband. For the last fifteen years she'd been doing sewing for women about town, and it was known that if she liked the woman she was sewing for she was capable of turning out a dress which had more fit and style to it than had that of any other seamstress in town. After being shown a design in a fashion magazine she could reproduce it with great skill. All she required was that her client sit and talk to her chummily for a while. With her broken accent she would recount stories of her past, and imagine great fortunes she was to inherit in the future. About Brick she worried little. "He tinks dot I'm dotty, my poy. Vell, he ain'd so far off, but I feeds him regular und he is a pright poy. Ernie (Brick's given name) vill look oud vor himself."

For various reasons Mrs. Simpson was held in some awe by both the young and adult people of town. For one thing she had a temper that could blaze and explode so that a victim of it might be forced to run down the street for more than a block with Mrs. Simpson in pursuit with a butcher knife, a flat iron, or some weighty weapon. Brick, impudent to her generally, had her moods delicately timed by now, so that he knew when to desist and slip out of the house, whereupon her memory lapsed. There were never aftermaths of her temper, for him, but for various townsmen of standing there was much aftermath.

At the time of the building of the Masonic Lodge, at least ten men had called upon Mrs. Simpson, individually, and in committees of two, three, or five men, in an endeavor to buy her lot and cottage so that they could do away with it. It was an eyesore, standing as it did right next to the supposedly beautiful Masonic Lodge. She was offered three times the value of her property; five times; ten times; but Mrs. Simpson would not sell out. It was too much trouble finding another place and moving her scant furniture. Another cottage was found her; a promise to move her belongings and add to her furniture was made. Mrs. Simpson stolidly refused to sell out. The end of the proposition was that the last committee which awaited upon her was received in fury, with Mrs. Simpson behind a barricaded door. Upon the table placed behind the door were her flat irons, a rolling pin, her kitchen ware, and some crockery, and she made it plain that she would not be slow at using them as projectiles if anybody tried to enter her house. She had no belief whatever in their intentions to do the best by her. A conviction had settled into her mind that they were trying to get her out of town, to do her out of her house and home, and to condemn her and Brick to the county poor farm. And in her mind there was no reason to believe that her shack was not a fitting companion dwelling for the Masonic Temple.

For over a year after this attempt Mrs. Simpson, standing in the doorway of her shack, would glower forbiddingly at most people who passed her door. Her squat figure stood plump down in its doorway; her teutonic face had a grim suspicious and obstinately fighting expression. Only now and then would that expression relax. For Mrs. Hardcutt, or the Hardcutt children; for any young man she saw about with Brick; and for what clients she consented to sew for, though they were few, as she was apt to tell any lady "you ged plump to hell oud of mein house mit yer damned seamstressing. I ain'd a needing to vork for mein living. I god mein place next to den Temple von der Masonics."

But by now upon discovering Ike Sorenson asleep and dead to the world with drunkenness upon her coal bags Mrs. Simpson no longer even grunted. The first time she was distrustful and tried waking him, until she recognized sincere, orthodox, and downright drunkenness, drunkenness that did not waver from its righteous state of intoxication for the glimmer of a second.

After the first time she would only glance at him whenever he sought sleep and refuge in her coalshed, and upon going back into the house would comment to Brick, if he was at home "dat fool Svede, he's litted up once more oud on de coalbags." By what instinct Ike, when drunk, knew that Mrs. Simpson's coalshed was permissible sanctuary one can not judge. He never saw her except when he was too drunk to see, and the two of them were never known to exchange a word with each other.

On this killingly hot summer afternoon, with heat lasting well after five o'clock with most of its repressed volcanic intensity, Dutchie McPherson started to the cow pasture a half mile from the edge of town. He had a job of driving the cows of three neighbors to and from pasture every morning and evening, and for each cow he was given fifty cents a week, so that the $1.50 he earned gave him a weekly fortune, to his ten year old mind. Going down Gander Street he felt that the air was cooling a little, but ominously. Perhaps it would rain, and that would cool things up somewhat. He didn't mind how hard it rained because he was barefoot and barelegged to his knees, with nothing on but a thin and very old shirt and a well worn pair of trousers.

At the edge of town he encountered Ike Sorenson who was staggering down the road, Dutch saw, after his team of horses which had started off without him. The horses were so used to going to Ike's farm with Ike dead to knowledge and ability to guide them, that they doubtlessly believed he was lying in the wagon in a drunken stupor. Dutchie ran after the wagon and stopped the horses until Ike came up. Ike was obstinate. He refused to mount the wagon seat. His three or four hour sleep at Mrs. Simpson's had done little to sober him, and of course he'd drunk more whiskey upon awakening. Dutchie knew there was no use trying to convince Ike of anything in such a state, so tying the horses to a tree by the side of the road, he left Ike, who by now had lain down in the roadside ditch near the wagon. Dutchie philosophically decided that with nobody around to be obstinate with, Ike would probably get into the wagon and drive off.

Heading towards the pasture again Dutchie went down the lane, and in. The three cows, used to him by sight, and knowing the time of day, had come up near the gate. They went out immediately and down the road towards their stables a half mile away. Dutchie was sure by the look of the sky that it was going to rain hard; even the cows seemed anxious to get home soon. It would probably be a great storm with thunder and lightning. Suddenly the water came. Dutchie had never experienced anything like it There wasn't a drop of water; there was a torrent falling in masses from the sky for a period of three to five minutes. It seemed that its weight would crush the breath out of him.

As suddenly as the water had come it ceased. All the road before Dutchie and the three cows, now sleek and drippingly shiny, was a river through which he must wade, nearly up to his knees in water. He felt dazed. This kind of phenomenon of nature was new to him, though he had known of tornadoes, and cyclones, and had seen a blizzard only the winter before. He was afraid that this might be just a prelude to a cyclone which he knew could create fearful havoc. The wind was beginning to whip through the trees so that a frenzy of twisting, bending, and squeaking noises commenced. A cloud went over the sun a minute; the rainbows were gone. He must get home quickly because if the wind came up strong, one of the trees along the roadside might break and fall upon him, or upon one of the cows.

Within ten minutes he was home, and had the cows in their stables. Whereupon he hastened to his own home. The wind was increasing; all of the orchard surrounding his family's house was billowing as though a tidal wave were sweeping through the earth beneath it and in the sky above. He heard a crash and saw that the great old elderwood tree across the road had broken its rotted trunk and was falling rippingly across the roadway. That would be dangerous for teams and automobiles which tried to pass through on this road, but there would probably be none, because for a long distance the sudden rush of water had gashed deep sluiced holes in the road, so that parts of the roadway were as deeply cut in as were the ditches on either side.

Not until he'd put on dry clothes and warmed himself by the kitchen fire did Dutchie recall old Ike Sorenson, whereupon he had a great twitch of fear and conscience. What if old Ike was drowned by the rush of water in the ditch where he'd been left sleeping. Or what if the tree to which the horses had been tied had broken and fallen upon them or Ike. Of course the horses would be panic struck, and might have trampled Ike, or dragged the wagon over him in an attempt to break away.

The next day, after the storm had subsided for over ten hours, and the report of small houses blown in, trees down, crops trampled by the rain and wind, had begun to come in, Dutchie found that none of his fears for old Ike had been realized. Apparently old Ike had just feigned sleep yesterday, as he always had to be perverse, and as soon as Dutchie had left him had climbed into his wagon and driven towards his farm hell-kapluting, because Farmer Graves had seen him galloping his horses down the road shamelessly. And when Mrs. McPherson called up Farmer Pyle, a near neighbor of Ike's, she found that he'd been home by seven o'clock the night before. People were always predicting that Ike would do himself to death with drink, or come to a violent death through recklessness, but the predictions had not come through in an eight year period. Some instinct appeared to guide him no matter how blind with liquor he might be.

For over a year the eight room house across from the Scotts' had been empty. Mrs. Scott often wished that it would be torn down as it was in such bad repair that surely no self-respecting family would move into it, since Deacon Pothatch was so tightfisted it could not be expected that he'd spend money on renovation. However a family was now moving in. Not much was known of them, the Angus family, except that the old man was a retired farmer, notable for honesty and the quickness with which he paid his bills amongst tradesmen.

However this was hardly the neighborhood for such a family, as it was about here that all the best Protestant people lived. The Ambersons, the Scotts, the Parkins, and the well established Jewish family, the Kramers. Of course many of the children of these families were grown up, or away at school, but the younger ones could hardly be playmates for the younger Angus girl. She'd be very lonely with children of twelve in sixteen so parents are not apt to take in a newcomer with a farm upbringing. Their furniture too, it could be noticed as it came up in vans, was most shabby.

Mrs. Colton, herself fairly new to the neighborhood, but the widow of a high school professor, first talked to Mrs. Angus across their backyard fence. She found Mrs. Angus to be a simple goodly soul; and when she took to buying her eggs and milk from Mrs. Angus and found it a convenience, Mrs. Scott, and the others also took to getting butter, eggs and milk there. Soon too, Carrie Colton, Alec Amberson, and Loraine Parkins, ventured an acquaintance with twelve year old Lucile Angus, because she had a croquet set on her lawn, and her parents made less fuss about the lawn being torn up than any of their parents did. Once or twice Lucile got petulant, and was ready to hit Alec Amberson with her croquet stick, or pouted and refused to play, but that all passed off. However when school came around they paid little attention to Lucile as she was so dubbish looking.

Lucile's older sister, Nellie, started going with Bert Thompson, a professional baseball player, and even he seemed too good for her. She was so countrified looking, and lolly. Before long it was evident that things had gone too far between Nellie and Bert, and Nellie went out of town. She was gone a month, and everybody was sure it was to be operated on to avoid having a child. When she returned she was pallid looking; and Bert Thompson saw no more of her. He was now going around with Winifred Downing, who belonged to a very good family, and had intelligence enough so that if she took Bert in hand she might make something out of him rather than just a roustabout. He had good stuff in him. Nellie stopped Bert on the street one day, and talked vehemently at him for almost an hour, but after that they avoided each other.

From now on Nellie began to dress much better than she had before, and she was continually on the streets. Too often she would be around the livery stable talking to men who hung around there. People ceased even to talk of her, it became so generally known that she would take on almost any man of however slight attraction; but she was pitied a little because it was supposed she was still violently in love with Bert Thompson and was only being desperate.

Again Nellie went away from town, and this time did not return for several months. Old man Angus, and her brother Jim, were wondered at for being so kindly tolerant of her looseness, but they seemed to have accepted the fact that she was over-passionate and unbalanced to such an extent that she must be allowed to go on her way. Perhaps she was not altogether normal. Her brother, Jim, particularly, was easy with her, considering the fact that he worked like an overburdened farmhand long hours every day on his father's four farms; and he rented other acres to plant in onions and potatoes. Jim was too gentle; too beaten; he seemed simply to drag himself through days expecting nothing whatever of existence for himself.

If he'd been a very religious man it would have been more understandable, but he was not that. Boys about town too, who worked occasionally making hay, picking potatoes, or husking corn, liked to work for him because he was so light a taskmaster, and paid them men's wages in spite of their youth.

When Nellie returned to town again she was much better dressed than before; as she stepped from the train, people at the station thought at first that a new and fashionable young lady had come to town, until she had gone most of the way down Egan Avenue to her home. Then she encountered Bert Thompson, and refused to stand talking to him after the first few greetings had been exchanged.

"Now Bert, you and I are through with each other. Let's just leave it that way. I would have done anything for you once . . . I was mad about you, but that's over. You look like a country bumpkin to me now," Nellie told Bert.

"Where've you been all this time? I've wondered often."

"In Chicago; I took up stenography."

"I'll call and get you tonight to talk over old times."

"No you needn't. I won't be in. We're through."

"What's the trouble?"

You treated me like a second rate whore once; what more do you want? In the city men at least show the girls they play around with a good time—they spend money. I'm off charity cases. Besides I'm reformed; I'm a good girl now. Like hell! But I know how to use the gimme's with you men at any rate. You stick by your little Winnie; she's your bet. I'm only passing through town, and when I leave I think I'll get a job in a chorus somewhere. My shape will get me by." Saying this Nellie went on down the street, leaving a puzzled Bert behind her. She'd developed a racy line of conversation; had taken to rouging and making up her eyes and lips. In passing she created the impression of style and beauty though she had no actual good looks, but Bert evidently desired to re-conquer a battle he'd thought permanently won. Now Nellie seemed to have gone further than he had, because she was no longer of the village, while he was doomed to it.

When the school term started at the high school there were several new teachers expected; there, as well as at the Normal. It had been decided that too many teachers had grown stagnant through long service in Wentworth, so many had been asked to resign the year before, and an effort had been made to get younger women, and men, fresh from college. Amongst them was the new Latin teacher, Miss Ridge, who was well over thirty however, but came so well recommended that she was accepted. She was a blackhaired, amazon-like woman with bitterly witty black eyes. Unable to locate a room elsewhere the first day she was in town she finally landed at the Angus home, where she intended to stay only long enough to locate otherwise, as they did not want a roomer.

Miss Ridge was later the terror of students in her classes. Her caustic irony, the slow curl of her lip and nostril as she handed out zeros to students she said were "bluffing," her quickness at discovering pupils who used ponies to help them translate their Latin, and the efficient sarcasm she dealt out to members of the school-board, as well as to Supt. May of the high school, made her a legend of grimness in town. Fond mammas found it difficult to explain to her the real precocity of their children to whom she'd given failing marks. Her purple-black eyes set in a square-jawed face could burn with too much jeering doubt.

Miss Ridge did not move from the Angus home; within a week of her arrival it was noticed that she was constantly around with Nellie Angus. Mrs. Lewis, capable of condemning any slight impropriety of action, found it difficult to give judgment here. Having conversed once with Miss Ridge, she'd learned that Miss Ridge was of an old Southern family, with a grandfather and a father who had both been notable men of science and surgery; and more, it struck Mrs. Lewis that Miss Ridge would not be a woman to wilt before any comment she might make. Of course as Miss Ridge was not properly of the town, Mrs. Lewis consoled herself, she need not give final judgment.

"The only way I can understand her friendship with that girl is that she does not know of the girl's past, and she's too much into books, and too intellectual to know what might be said of her. Some one must inform her I'm sure," Mrs. Lewis talked. But no one informed Miss Ridge of Nellie's past; no one became that familiar with her; and the quick way she slaughtered any bit of town scandal whispered to her made it difficult. Apparently she really liked Nellie Angus however, because they were together constantly except for the hours when Miss Ridge was at school.

Later it proved that Miss Ridge was a rampant feminist; carrying aloft the blazing banner of equal rights, economically and morally, for her sex. She horrified an entire roomful of women at a club meeting by delivering a speech justifying the woman libertine, condemning the prostitutionalism of the marriage relationship, and insisting upon the moral duty of all women of the so-called upper classes to spread the gospel of birth control. In delivering her speech, she whipped herself into a fury of eloquence which, had any men been present, might have effectively driven them from town as from a scourge. She was terrific and terrifying in her conviction of the injustice to her sex which had lasted through all the ages.

Nellie Angus stayed in town the whole school year. Any tendency which she might have had to cringe before townspeople was eradicated by the fire of Miss Ridge's eloquence; Nellie took colour, defiance, and insolence of manner from Miss Ridge. Men she'd formerly consorted with were passed by, looked through, and ignored; girls about town she was completely indifferent to, but it was noted that both she and Miss Ridge were out of town over almost every week-end, and what these trips might mean—with a woman thinking what Miss Ridge thought—

Summer vacation came around again, and with it Miss Ridge departed, having decided not to return another year to Wentworth.

Within a week after her departure Nellie Angus was gone from town too, and was not heard from for some time, when it was discovered that she was at the University of Chicago, taking what special courses her previous scanty education permitted. Two years later it was reported that she d married a wealthy widower with two children; a man who was in politics in a small way—alderman, or some such thing.

Because of the departure of the Freeman, the Fitzgerald, the Warden, and other children, now grown up, of the better families in town, into marriage, business, or into the decay of old-maidism, and because of the exuberant young gaiety of life about in all the younger generation, a few families now began to emerge as the staid and tried aristocracy of the village. For some unknown reason the Degens were one of the families so respected; perhaps the reason being that having wealth they still lived a detached life. Be that as it may, scandal enough had in the past been about regarding the thirty-year-old Bert Degen, and his nearly half-witted sister.

Bert was a heavy set, sullenly handsome, but completely lethargic, individual with rude manners, and little wit, which his arrogance and pomposity made seem even less than it was. It was probable that his marriage to Adelaide Compson two years before had to take place sooner than either intended as their baby was born shortly after their marriage; but that was not the whispered scandal. It was said that years before, Bert, with other young boys of sixteen, among them Tom Warden, had seduced his younger sister, who never seemed quite right mentally; he and Tom Warden were of much the same type, as were their wives. Edith Warden however, at one time Edith Burton, while having the same black-haired, overflushed complexion, small dark-eyed type of striking looks that people who admired wealth chose to call beauty, had at least a wit of a sort, and more generosity. Adelaide Degen tried to carry off a grand manner on the strength of a nasty disposition.

Doubtlessly it was the oldest girl, Gay Degen, who most estab-

lished the family as one of exceptionally good standing in Wentworth; for she was a brilliant pianist, had lived much in Chicago
and New York, and was the first person known to go to Europe
from the community, and she had lived three years in Paris. When
she returned she refused to teach music, but went instead to a
physical culture training school and became an athletic instructor
simply to occupy her time. A small, wispish person who looked as
if the skin were drawn too tightly about her pale face, she had a dry
sense of humour, and a poise come from indifference, that made
her respected; and she steadily refused to pretend to like her
brother, or her sister-in-law; and claimed any idea that family
relationships signified much, ridiculous. How could it be possible,
that simply because they were related to her by blood, Bert and his
wife could mean anything to her, when their chief pleasures were
playing bridge, autoing, and going to moving pictures, and being
with people whose main conversation was indulging in off-colour
jokes. No, she'd travel; and her parents could come along with her
when they chose, or better still, they could travel alone, to places
she recommended, and perhaps Agnes, the witless sister, might
with middle age and much travelling experience, prove more of a
person than she was now. Some girls mature slowly.

The Downing girls too, were coming into their day now. With
the death of their father they immediately began to emerge. It
hadn't been evident to an outsider's eye that he was rigid with
them, for he seemed completely jovial and tolerant, but now it
appeared he'd nursed some constant fear that they would lose their
reputations and run wild unless he held the reins on them tightly.
So even Winifred Downing, at thirty, had a blossoming forth,
though she still went with Bert Thompson and eventually married
him. She was a dark mouselike person, who seemed discouraged
about things from the beginning, as neither she nor her second
sister Elsie were deemed pretty. The growing up of Leila possibly
was the means by which the two older girls re-blossomed, for after
Leila's fifteenth year she was spoken of for some six years as the
most popular girl in town. At eighteen she went to Chicago, to the

97

same physical training school that Gay Degen had gone to. She went a slim, mildly pretty, blue-eyed girl with chestnut-coloured hair; and her sisters followed her to take the same course. Ten months later they all returned, gayer, with much style, and— particularly Leila—much vivacity; a manner that didn't ask for attention, but which simply assumed that she would get it, and so she got it. Within the year she'd filled out, learned fancy dancing, and become almost boisterously a good fellow. Her tall figure, which was rather big-hipped, could be seen at balls, dancing with great gaiety every dance on the program. Her pale hair which she had learned how to arrange, her violet blue eyes, and boldly frank face, which had liveliness in it, came to be called beautiful simply because of cocksure, hail-fellow, mannerisms. Then other girls began to declare that she was nothing but bluff, and that she gained her popularity amongst men simply by her fellowship actions, and her pretended indifference to conventions, though actually she was more conservative than many other girls in town. There wasn't nearly as much gameness in her as there was in her older sisters, who became mildly popular along with her, as they resembled her slightly, danced well, and—it proved—in spite of their twenty-seven and thirty years, were quite ready to pet and cuddle with young men as much as ten years younger than they. They perhaps were surer of their ability to stop at the right moment than the more cautious Leila.

The two Scott girls, Madge and Lillian, never got into the tradition of gameness, as the younger generation considered it. Mrs. Scott was too austere in her bringing-up of them; she taught them music from the time they were four years old, and insisted upon her parental authority. They were both grave, studious individuals anyway, and perhaps would on their own impulses have drifted into spending more time reading than at anything else. The Scott library was full of girls' books; and boys' books that Lloyd and his younger brother, Walter, had. The Elsie books; Louisa M. Alcott's works; Jane Austen; Jack Harkaway; the Alger books; Henty; Cooper; etc. They were unusual in being the kind of girls that Jane Austen might have written about, except that no social proprieties existed about them to function upon them so surroundingly as around Jane Austen's young ladies. So they were simply reserved for their environment.

Living near the Scotts were the Coltons. Mrs. Colton was a little robust in her humour at times, for Mrs. Scott's taste; and Mr. Colton's red face and matted fleshiness showed his taste for drink too, while he almost constantly, when not in the house, had his mouth full of a great wad of chewing tobacco; but when either he or his wife were too boisterous or vulgar, Mrs. Scott, knowing their good nature, and that they had come from good parent stock, would simply say "Now Jennie"—or "Now Jim," and the matter would be laughed off. Carrie Colton particularly had inherited her mother's tomboyishness and skittishness, and with it a fresh bossy manner which respected no elders, and which made her ready to burlesque or do a slapstick comedy imitation of anybody in town. The Colton boys simply weren't; John was a girlboy, and liked to skip the rope at fourteen, or play the piano, or sew; Walter was a dumbhead who at eighteen had not been able to get through the eighth grade at school, or write a sentence of ten words rightly spelled. He could drink, and raise the devil about town however, which gave him a standing with the younger generation, while his brother was simply a person to be joked about.

Henry Scott, while at the garage preparatory to driving his auto into the country on a tour to inspect his three farms, remarked to his younger boy, Walter, that he'd better take the cow out to Daly's dairy farm. "She won't give any milk at all if we don't let her have another calf soon," he declared.

Billy Hardcutt had come over to find Walter and see if there wasn't some way for them to pass away a desultory summer's day. He thought they might walk out to Lake Borrows three miles from town and have a swim there; or perhaps they could hunt birds' eggs in the woods on the edge of town.

"Come on Billy, let's take the damned cow out to Daly's," Walter said. "It won't take more'n a couple of hours there and back and maybe we'll see some birds' nests in the trees along the country road."

Taking the undersized Jersey cow, which was obstinate in her moods, the boys started down the street with her. She led docilely except that she wanted to browse upon the beautifully kept lawn of warmest green grass that was in front of the Scott house. They persuaded her away from that however and walked down a cross-road to the main country road. It was but a mile to Daly's farm. A clear shimmer of blue and sunlight pervaded the spaces all about, and the odour of alfalfa from fields they passed came to the boys' nostrils. A slow breeze was blowing across the wheat and cornfields along the roadside; from the telephone wires strung between tall posts at twenty yard intervals came a humming song.

Daisy, the cow, walked along complacently, not at all disposed to hurry her pace at moments of impatience which came to the boys. However as she came to the edge of the pasture in which the Daly cows browsed she balked somewhat, seeming to sense too well what she was going into and to feel the need of acting reluctant.

An eighth mile away across the pasture most of the herd of cattle were browsing or reclining upon the grass chewing their cuds; others stood knee deep in the fragrant marsh pond, chewing lily pads, or simply standing to have the wetness on their legs. Seeing a strange cow approaching down the road, Othello, the bronze bull, who was accustomed to having cows brought him, came running across the pasture to the fence. Daisy insisted upon getting to him on the other side of the fence. She and Othello smelled noses, whereupon Daisy tossed her head with an impatient gesture. It took a good deal of strength to pull her away and lead her down the road to the entrance of the Daly farm, but they contrived to do so. Mrs. Daly, who was rocking a barrel churn out on the front veranda of the farm house, looked self-conscious, and informed the boys that they'd find her husband at the cow stable. Soon he appeared, and helped them lead Daisy into the small pasture where Othello now was.

Daisy was obstinate; she would not stand still; did not want anything to do with Othello, though Walter remarked she'd obviously been in heat since yesterday. "She never wants to take it anyway. She always has to be forced," he told Mr. Daly.

"Some females are that way," Mr. Daly joked, "We'll just thrust the lady into the serving pen. Lead her here."

Once Daisy was inside the serving pen, which was so narrow she could not twist away, the act of service was accomplished, though Daisy bent her back into such a cramped position that Mr. Daly thought the service might not have taken, and waited until Othello wished to try again. A sour look of distaste showed on Daisy's bovine countenance, as if she wished to throw up, and thought the whole procedure disgusting to her higher cow nature.

"That'll take I guess," Mr. Daly asserted," but watch her next month and see if she comes into heat again. If she does bring her out. There's some cows can throw it out of them. Funny they act that way too, because it's them that are bulliest in the pasture when there's no male around. Now if she was like a little brown heifer that I'm keeping in the pasture for Mr. Granger I wouldn't want her around. That young heifer uses the bulls up. She's taken on Othello and the two yearling bulls every day for the three weeks she's been here. The other cows refuse to have anything to do with her she's so improper."

Walter and Billy laughed and looked sheepish. Both, being but thirteen years old, weren't used to being talked to so frankly by older men, as though they understood everything and there was nothing to be self-conscious about. Snickering, they led Daisy out of the pasture and down the road on the way home. She was decidedly moody now, and refused at one moment to budge; on a sudden impulse she decided to trot until suddenly she stopped short and refused to budge again. Pull as both of them might on the sides of her halter not one step would she move. Then quickly, after having planted her front feet to brace herself against their strength, she lifted up her tail and started into a gallop that was so rapid neither of the boys could have run so fast alone. They held on however, knowing that it might take an hour to catch her if she got away. Down the road at a tremendous pace the three of them tore, until Walter and Billy were completely exhausted in their lungs, legs, and arms. Daisy was even dragging them so that their feet no longer stepped at some moments. By the time she had run a quarter of a mile however she calmed down again, and while temperamental the rest of the way home, she did not get out of control, so that in a half hour she was in her pasture back of the Scott barn.

That afternoon Walter and Billy encountered Mr. Daly on the town streets. "Do one of you boys want a job of a month or so with me?" he asked them. "You can milk I take it, and could do a few light chores to help the hired man who's busy plowing corn this season."

Walter's father, who was the most successful attorney in Wentworth, wasn't likely to let him take the job, but Billy knew he could, and was glad of the chance of earning a few dollars for himself, though that would mean that Walter would get ahead of him on his bird egg collection probably. He made arrangements to be out at the Daly farm to stay the next morning.

Mr. and Mrs. Daly were alien spirits in Wentworth. They'd come ten years back, and for eight years Mr. Daly was the village jeweler and watch repairer, working in the McKinnon Drug Store. Evidently he was of better class than his occupation indicated, and better educated than most men about town; or evidently he himself thought so, the others believed. Certainly he presented a more tailored front before he became a dairyman, and his manners were more suave. His curly dark hair, clear blue eyes, and round, rosy, but goodfeatured face had a quality of boyish naïveté in it, but there was aloofness in him towards most people in town, so that ten years had not served to make him and his wife particularly friendly with anybody.

Two years before this time Mr. Daly, who for some time had been buying registered Jersey cattle, had gone into the dairy business forsaking the jewelry trade. He borrowed sufficient capital to get on mortgage a ten acre ranch a quarter of a mile from the edge of town, and here he increased his herd of cattle. Specializing in Jersey cows, and charging more for milk because of its richness, he managed to get most of the wealthier people in town as milk clients and also shipped to two city hotels. However his credit by now was distinctly bad all over town, for instead of paying his bills he was disposed to take trips and return with highly bred cows and calves for which he'd paid five to ten times the price of ordinary cattle. Everybody said he'd go broke sooner or later, indulging so much as he did in fads about farm fixtures, high class stock, and stable conveniences.

Mrs. Daly was a small, grave faced woman, with a Chinese quality in her white countenance. Upon the coming of the Public Library to Wentworth she had been made librarian, since she was surely the best read woman about town ready to take the job, and as a married woman, would work for a small salary. Before marrying Mr. Daly she had taught school elsewhere, and later served as a substitute teacher in the high school whenever sickness or other cause on the part of other instructors made her presence necessary. Working only afternoons and evenings at the library now, she managed to have time yet to do a good deal of work around the dairy farm, though the strain of the work told on her.

The first day that Billy Hardcutt worked at the farm went well for him, as he was enthusiastic about his new job, particularly about the part which meant caring for the calves. He listened eagerly to Mr. Daly's theories about stock raising, and proved more ready to measure out balanced rations, and to weigh the milk output of each cow, than any farmhand Mr. Daly had ever had.

The fifth evening Mrs. Daly stayed home from the library, as it was Saturday night and her substitute was acting. She knew Billy well before he'd come to the farm, for he'd taken many books from the library, and asked her questions about what to read. She'd started him reading Dickens, Thackeray, Eliot, and other books, rather than Jesse James stories or dime novels.

"Another night, if you like," Mrs. Daly told Billy, "we can read aloud to each other. I haven't indulged in that lately. Mr. Daly has too little time, though he and I have both been wanting to get to *Little Dorrit*, or to some George Meredith book, for the last year. But this new business of farming uses up all our energy. I don't know whether it will make us happier or not, but then as we have no children, and apparently won't have, it's best to keep busy I suppose."

Billy said nothing, sensing a sadness in Mrs. Daly, who he knew, from remarks she'd made to his sister, wanted children. The night was calm with country quietness, marked by the distant humming of innumerable mosquitoes which circled conelike over the swamp down in the cow pasture. It was eight o'clock, and still clear enough to read without a lamp had one wished. Crickets sang from the fields about.

"I wonder what I'll really do when I grow up," Billy mused. "I can't think the same thing for long. I think now I'd like to raise Jersey cows; I like them. They're so intelligent for cows, but I guess I like horses best at that. I'd like to raise everything, but of course I don't know where I'd get the money."

"But Ralph didn't know where he'd get it either; it simply takes daring, though perhaps he's too daring and doesn't look further ahead than a dream or a fad sometimes. He's always been that way since I knew him."

"When did you first know him?"

"That—it is shocking I suppose, or people would think they must believe it so, because everything connected with our marriage was unconventional. Ralph, after finishing preparatory school in the East didn't want to go to college though his parents wanted him to go to Princeton. So he just took a job with a travelling carnival. When he passed through the town I lived in he was selling knickknacks from a booth, in front of which I stopped one day. Our eyes met for just a minute, but I didn't think much about it except that he was a very nice looking young man to be on a job of that kind. But five minutes later a boy handed me a note from Ralph, asking me if I would permit him to introduce himself. Of course I thought that rather impudent, but then I realized he wouldn't know anybody I knew to introduce us, and if he wanted to meet me—well, I let him come and talk to me. And as a result, here we are, married for twelve years now. Of course marriages that take place in that way might be terribly disastrous, but I think I knew pretty well after the first conversation that Ralph was no ordinary circus man."

"Gosh, if he were, he couldn't be any worse than some of the men the women around this town are married to. I don't see how people go on living as stupid as some of them are. They don't want anything but their meals out of life. I know I'll have to get something more than they do if I go on," Billy said.

Mrs. Daly listened with rather tired sympathy to Billy as he talked, now full of ideas about what he wanted to do, and where he wanted to go. Finally, musing, she commented:

"Of course I don't know what I would have done, who I would have married, if Ralph hadn't come along, and I don't suppose it would have made much actual difference about how I feel about life now. So long as one is interested about how things are going on, or in having them go on, that is enough. There are times though when so many things have to be solved, and other times— nothing. My sister Kitty, with her two children, seems happier than me, but she has always asked less. Not that I'm unhappy—" she added reflectively. "I don't know. I can't be as interested in the dairy farm as Ralph is, I wouldn't be here except that he's so pleased with the thought that some day it will be a model place, and I hope he manages that with all the hope and energy he's putting into it. But the debts are piling up. I'm sure he owes thousands more now than everything we possess would ever bring, because nobody around here cares whether cattle are high-priced, registered stock or not."

Mr. Daly, who after milking, separating, and bottling the milk, had driven to town to deliver it over the route, came back by nine fifteen, having made an exceptionally quick trip this evening.

"I tell you Annie, I'm feeling cheered up," he told his wife. "Not one creditor stopped me tonight, and Mr. Fitzgerald, the hardware man, whom I owe from months back, said he was glad to see a man with so much pride about improving his place as I have. We'll be out of our financial tangles within two years, if not less, and once out, we can stand clear with the ranch and stock worth fifteen to twenty five thousand dollars. Nothing risked, nothing gained. I've been thinking as I drove home that I'd get rid of those few prize hogs Mr. Irish left on my hands when he sold us the ranch. I'll just put an ad in some farm journal with a snappy headline, say *Hogs Do Not Pay situated as I am*, and so on. Once rid of those hogs I can concentrate on high class cattle and you can go on with your chickens if you wish. I mean not to have one head of cattle on this ranch that isn't thoroughbred as soon as I can afford to have it so."

Billy listened, warmed by Mr. Daly's enthusiasm and becoming increasingly eager to learn all he could about cattle raising on a scientific basis. It pleased his vanity to know that Mr. Daly had told his wife he thought him the brightest youngster he'd ever known, and more to be trusted to see a job done in the right way than any hired man. Billy wondered to himself at one moment if his own interest would hold on through, nevertheless, as he remembered the Chautauqua season would be on at Lake Borrows in a week, and he'd miss all that while Walter Scott, Bob McPherson, and other boys would be swimming, boating, and playing around. That fear lasted only a moment however because he did think the cows such beautiful creatures, and he was sure they had more affection for him than they had even for Mr. Daly who didn't pet them as he did.

Every day however did not go as well as the first five days had. Sometimes Mr. Daly would arrive back from town in the morning, or in the evening, and be full of curses about the avarice and narrow-mindedness of townspeople in Wentworth. A woman client may have failed to pay her milk bill for two months or more;

another might have said she didn't find Jersey cows' milk any better than ordinary cows; a creditor may have become insistent upon the payment of a bill; or some man have joshed him on his newfangled ideas on farming, taunting him with the insinuation that they didn't pay for themselves.

"Christ almighty," he confided to Billy, with whom he talked more than he did to the illiterate farmhand he was forced to employ for heavier work, "you would think that it was immoral or a crime to deviate a little bit to talk to some of those mossbeards in town. They're red-eyed if anybody shows a little originality or initiative. What in hell is it to them if I choose to keep a clean stable and have the udders of my cows washed before they're milked. There's old Pete Olson on the other side of town trying to ridicule me. I'd be ashamed to have as much cowdung in a pail of my milk as he gets into every bottle of his. They want to scoff at me because I think. You'd believe yourself an outcast for being called a gentleman farmer to hear them talk. Any of the wealth anybody in that town has he has simply because it was thrown at him by a town growing up around land he bought years back, and lived a hog upon, no doubt."

Billy assented and was silent, unable to be as vehement in his assent to Mr. Daly's bitterness as Mr. Daly was himself. After a lapse Mr. Daly took up again:

"What I want to know is how they can blame a man for not having children? It's not the man's fault. Of course amongst cattle a bull gets impotent at periods, but that's because of too much corn fodder. It's a matter of feed. Jesus Christ, when I come in from town sometimes I feel like throwing the whole thing up and getting a position as supervisor to some wealthy man's model farm in the east. A man works his hands off here, but who cares? Suppose I make this thing go in a few years' time amongst these people, what will I have that I want? and I'll have gone to seed too."

Two and half months passed, and it was near time for Billy to be starting to school for the fall term again. He had as yet received no money for his work, and felt disappointed because several times he'd wanted money when amongst other boys in town of an evening. However he said nothing to Mr. Daly, who lately had been more and more worried about his state of affairs. Billy felt sorry for Mrs. Daly, since through the hot summer months she'd become frailer looking constantly, and during a period when ten new cattle were being shipped to Mr. Daly from an auction sale he'd attended, she worked every day from five o'clock in the morning until eleven o'clock at night, at the ranch, except for the hours she was at the library. Plainly she and her husband were simply dragging through existence, meaning little to each other in the way of companionship or of encouragement, as they no longer had any evident interest in each other. In the last few weeks Mr. Daly's idea that he rid himself of the ranch and all the cattle was repeated many times, and he was apparently looking for a prospective buyer. His creditors were forcing him.

It was not however until six months later that he was finally forced to declare himself bankrupt. The ranch and its stock were sold at auction. For some months after he and his wife lingered about town, living on borrowed money and the few dollars a month Mrs. Daly earned, and then they left, as Mr. Daly had secured a position as farm manager in the east. He was not heard of for about a year, when it was found that he then had a position caring for the stables at a State Insane Asylum, which institution conducted a dairy farm to employ the least affected of its patients. Mrs. Daly was in Chicago taking a course in librarianship so that she could command a higher salary than she'd received in Wentworth, and it was doubted that she and her husband would actually live together again, though there seemed to be no definite break between them.

Thomas Campbell having failed to make much of a success as an attorney in a small town in Kentucky, moved to Kansas City; after five years there he again moved, this time to Wentworth. Money his wife had received on a small inheritance helped this second move. The family, made up of seven children, had at this time been in the village but eight months.

People who wished to speak well of Mr. Campbell would say that at least he was a godly man; he was a constant church-goer, and rigid with his family in their observances of the gospel truths as he interpreted them. So when he discovered that his nineteen-year-old son was playing pool with other young men of the town at the billiard hall he came home in a righteous fury; adding to his fury was his knowledge of the report that John was misbehaving with a town girl of bad character.

John, sullen always towards his father, met his fury with an insolent indifference. In the morning he had been at his father's office doing some typing for him. Then he'd felt caged; and upon his face was such an expression as a chained wolf might wear; a look that told of his desire to be away; a look a young male animal, for the moment tyrannized over by an older male animal but still rebellious inwardly, might wear. As he had typed he wondered what family could mean to him; or what hold his father had upon him; hadn't he better just get off and go away. He could make his living as a farm hand at least if at nothing else; or he could save money off some farm job for a few months, and then go to the city and try locating there. Of course the farmers around here would work the hide off him, and they were inclined to think his hands too soft, and his frame too slight. Still labourers were scarce about.

Having fretted within himself all day, when his father came upon him now in the back yard he was in no mood to be respectful.

"Yes I've been playing pool. What sin is there in that? What in the devil do you think? You bring us to a one horse town like this to live and expect me to sit around and twiddle my fingers," he answered his father.

The end of it was that his father had taken a horsewhip and struck him twice, before he caught the whip and jerked it away, shouting, "By Christ you won't touch me with a horsewhip again or you'll get it used on you." He was white to the lips, and looked as though he were going to strike his father, but his mother who had heard the argument got between them and clung to John, finally persuading him to go into the house. He hesitated a moment on the stairway before going up, and then ascended to his room and began to pack his clothes into a bundle. Evidently his mother sensed his intention for she was at his door when he come out.

"You're not going away, John," she pleaded in maternal terror. "Not in this temper."

"I have to go. There's no use. I won't stand it anymore, and I don't see why you will."

His mother clung to him. "But wait anyway until after Thanksgiving; only three days. Your father will be sorry about his temper even if he is too stubborn to admit it. Please, John, stay for your mother's sake." His mother was weak as she clung to him, and he could sense the helplessness of despair in all her emotions.

A suspended pity was in him; a suspended disgust. How cold he felt towards her, towards everything, everybody. The damned obscenity of life. Even now he could almost be brutal enough to brush her aside and walk coldly away. There wasn't the possibility of a tender emotion in him at this moment. However he turned, saying "All right, but the day after Thanksgiving I go. I don't understand why you think I gain by simply staying around with you and the rest of the family. Your caring about me doesn't do anything for me, or make it easier to stand that damned hypocrite—I detest calling him father."

His mother tried to press John to her maternally, and to kiss him. He almost averted his lips. A nausea of physical contact possessed him. Why should he, how could he pretend an emotion, except a disgust of existence, and pity for his mother which added to that disgust and swept every other emotion out of his being. He went, with his face turned away, back into his room, and soon went out of the house saying that he would not eat dinner at home that night.

The three days till Thanksgiving passed with John carefully avoiding any conversation with his father; he came to meals at the last minute, bolted his food, and left the table immediately. His father said nothing further to him, for he realized that John was stronger than he, and a physical fear of his son had come into him.

Thanksgiving day came. Bessie Campbell spent all the morning in the kitchen preparing food. The cranberry jelly was stiff and clear; the plum pudding, only part of which she'd served today as it would be better being older at Christmas time; and the young, tender turkey, would make the dinner a success from that standpoint. She was glad guests were coming in to dinner as it would force John and his father to act friendly to each other, and that might mean their quarrel would pass over. John at least wasn't a nasty tempered boy, she thought to herself.

He came into the kitchen. "It's only nine thirty mother; we won't have dinner till after one will we?" he asked.

"Not until two if the Coltons are late at all," his mother answered.

"I think I'll go out and tramp in the fields then; take my gun with me and perhaps shoot a jack rabbit that we can have for supper tomorrow," he told her, and a few minutes later was gone out of the back door. A moment's anxiety came to Bessie; she didn't like there being a gun in the household and John was still feeling glum over the quarrel he'd had with his father, but he had said a 'rabbit we can have tomorrow night' so he wasn't thinking too much about going away from home at once.

Occupied with her food preparations Bessie dismissed anxiety from her mind after a few minutes. Her slight figure for all its frailty occasional full of energy that did not break under all her duties, caring for the entire routine of the household.

John Campbell went past cornfields late autumn crisped. Their leaves rasped and shuddered in the wind, and their stalks whined from the frost that kept them brittly chilled. A sere chill was within him too, a hard rebellion at life, rotted only in some portion of his heart where the weakness of despair was a warm fluid dampening the hardness of his defiance to helplessness.

Alternate waves of rage at, and indifferent understanding of, his father, flowed through him. At moments he felt he could almost sympathize with what life had made the older man. It was this very sympathy that made him feel helpless himself in all of his outlook on existence. At angry moments he could hatingly see his father's face within his mind, a face with waxen shiny eyes, insistent with neurotic rage. How dared he, having messed up his own life, as he had, presume to dictate to anybody else what they should or should not do as though he had discovered a right way, and knew always that what his son was doing was wrong.

But at the ebb of an emotion he would understand again. Who could retain temper or patience with the continual bickerings of family life, and forever pressing economic needs? Often enough John felt himself driven wild with the oppression of home life. What way was there to smash down all the barriers and have a degree of freedom to act, and if the impulses he had were sinful who had made them so? But what was he to do? He'd hate farm work; he'd hate office work in the city and despise the people working around him for their clerkish acquiescence. What was life about? A sickness of it was in his stomach, tiring him to complete non-resistance for the time being.

In fatigue and disgust of rebellion he recalled his dream last night, in which he had been walking in a meadow filled with the live bodies of people he could scarcely avoid trampling on. They had all evaporated as he tried to touch them with his hand. Half awake later, with his mind and impulses flooded with sex-desiring images, vapours had swirled vertiginously about, whirling and swooping him into themselves so that he felt a floating, dull, smothered, vapour himself, and a vapour pulsing with frustrated desire. Might he not as well have done with all life right now? Yes, he could go away; he could put himself through college, but he could not want to do that. Where were there people who could mean much to him? He'd observed enough lives not to believe anybody got much he'd want out of living.

Well, he could shrug this mood off, but it would recur. It might be a mood only, but the clarity and decision with which it made futility apparent, wracked him. There'd have to be a world far different from any that his experiences had encountered for him to care much. But why question? Why care? Leave it all unanswered. There was nothing painful in this present moment, of walking in the wind, gun in hand, not actually wanting to shoot a rabbit, but occupied with the idea and passing time away. Somehow time passed away, and when it was passed the most painful episodes in it seemed to have left little enough impression. So much of all that had happened in his life had merged into his mystification of being, so that many moments his senses were dazed with a bewilderment of trying to believe reality, that life is, that anything so ridiculous as sex actually is as it is, and that being so there is any restraint about it.

Exhilaration however had come into him as he walked in the wind with his strong buoyant stride bucking each gust and going through it so that it seemed one plate of wind after another breaking against him and falling to flatness. He was strong; he could enjoy the strength of himself. The moment's physical vanity of being began to make him animallically ecstatic; as a young bison on the prairies; or as a young wolf leading a pack. He knew he was beautiful to look at. He liked feeling that the sunlight was pursuing him to shed its warmth upon him in the midst of the crisp chill about. And the wind and cold was bringing higher colour to his face, and giving his eyes a cold grey tint. He felt his youngness, his vitality of resistance that was, and for this time would be, insistently proud and reckless of all thought. People! None of them could matter to him. He didn't need, like his father, to be disturbed about worshipping a god to have an after life. Somewhere else, another time, amongst other people, he would be—

He started whistling to himself, then singing, as his stride lifted him with a flying buoyancy along the path by the fence of the cornfield. The cornstalks were marching diagonally across the windblown fields, frost dampened soil glistening between them, reflecting their waving brown banners, glistening the sunlight back at the sun. Misery was suspended within him; a physical joy of being alone had him as the sun, now warm, now cold, mouthed him as it breathed through the wind. But still, submerged, a distaste at the necessity of returning home to live combatting his father's tyranny, made an impatience of life rooted deeply beneath this animal rhapsodic response to the moment.

As Bessie Campbell went on with the dinner preparations she was remembering other Thanksgivings and years, with the circumstances which had surrounded them. How differently she had conceived her future twenty years ago.

Aaron Workman, her father, had been an austere, god-fearing man, but there had always been kindliness beneath his uncommunicative exterior. He had insisted, only as all respectable families in the Scotch Kentucky community where his family lived, upon rigid church observances, family prayer morning and evening, and much church-going. But those younger years had been happy ones, it seemed now to Bessie. There'd been many people dropping in of an evening, and on Sundays, as her father's farmhouse was known as one with hospitable doors. There would be hymn singing; the singing of old melodies and school songs, the discussion of books, and harmless gossip when young people only were around; and generally a discussion upon some theological point between her father and his visitors when older people had called. To his place came every visiting minister, probably for lodging during his sojourn in the community, but at least for a meal or so. And there'd been many fewer quarrels between her and her brothers and sisters than seemed to take place now between her sons and daughters; but it was Thomas with his temper who had started that family custom.

A flux of impatience at her children, and the way they bound her, pulsed within Bessie for a moment, but an impulse of pride swept that impatience from her. It was wonderful to think that she had carried within her and borne John, and Isabel, and the others too, though they were younger and less magnificent to watch developing at the moment; except baby Irene; she would be as bright as the two older ones.

But yet her affections and imagination strained towards the past, as she wondered if she mightn't have had a happier life if she'd not married Thomas, but had instead simply stayed with her brother Kenneth always, because he and she had so completely understood each other in those younger years. She thought with a pang of regret of the time between her eighteenth and twenty-second year, when she'd lived alone with her younger brother Kenneth as he was improving a section of raw land which his father gave him. Kenneth's dependence on her had been pleasing, and he had always listened to her advice.

But of course she was proud seeing her own children through. Still she felt like weeping because of her tender memories. That Thanksgiving day when she and John were alone on his ranch: How well she recalled his coming into the shack from his morning chores. She'd carefully concealed the homespun suit she'd been working on for two weeks, and knew also that he had some surprise present for her. A palpitation of anticipation was in her for this was the first Thanksgiving either of them had ever spent away from home. As Kenneth came in he had all her affection. His inability to throw off his sense of responsibility about the farm and let the day be an easy one had touched her sympathies, but she hadn't known how to express her affection for him easily.

"It's too bad you're working just to get fancy things for me to eat, Bessie," Kenneth said. "I'd as soon had the regular fare. But now we will make a day of it between us and be all stuffed up." He went fumblingly about the room, and Bessie guessed that he was wanting to get into his box to take out some present for her. To give him the opportunity she went into the shack's second room, and in a minute came out with a suit she'd made him.

"Here is something for you to put on, Kennie, so we'll feel like company to each other," she said.

"You made it. Great stuff I'm thinking," Kenneth answered, shy about expressing his gratitude. "And you might put on what's in that package on your chair too."

Picking up the package Bessie found within it a black satin dress trimmed with white lace. She smiled to herself, flooded with tenderness for Ken, for his intention and for his not knowing that at twenty she wouldn't be wanting to wear the same kind of black satin dress her mother wore. She put the dress on and pinned on its breast a massive cameo brooch he'd given her once before, and then she served dinner. Before they started eating she served each of them a glass of blackberry wine made in the early fall. They both felt quite happy and talked freely of what the others would be doing at the old homestead.

"I'm glad we didn't leave the stock to drive twenty miles just to be at home. It's nice being alone this one Thanksgiving as long as it's you, Bessie," Kenneth said. "There'd be such a crew of relatives with the older ones, and their youngsters, and Nellie's husband, that I'm not liking too well. It's not much we'd get out of being there with the mob around."

Later they were planning a trip to take next year, or the year after, if Ken's crops came on well. "And even if it's not so good a year I'll take you, because it's coming to you, doing all my work and asking nothing for it."

"Aren't you my baby brother?" Bessie asked him. "I guess I can take care of you as well as I used to when I had to pull your ears for trying to play hookey from school."

"You always were a good boss all right. But we never scrapped much, did we? I think we're better off living this way than the others with all their family troubles and wranglings."

"We're well away from that sort of thing, for some years, and father will see that we don't need to worry about money even if the crops aren't so good for a year or so," Bessie answered. "It doesn't look now as though either of us are going to get married right away, but if you marry I'll be stranded, and a lonely old maid, because I couldn't live with any of the others. The old folks won't last so many years now."

"Don't you think I'll marry and leave you for a long time, not until after you do, and you can know I'm not looking forward to that. In a year or so we'll put up a house on this place that will make father's look pretty worn out," Kenneth answered.

So that Thanksgiving day had passed, and it had seemed then to Bessie that she would never want to alter her condition. In the spring however, because of her mother's illness she went home to stay and lingered to help about the house through her mother's convalescence and then it was she met Thomas Campbell, who was much in favour with her father because he was so religious a young man. Bessie hadn't thought much about him, except that he was weak looking, and at first she didn't like the look in his eyes which were pale brown and too intense. But when her father suggested him as a husband she looked at him differently. There was no gainsaying that he was fine looking; his small mouth was sensitive; his large, well carved nose denoted another class of breeding than that of people she was used to seeing about, and of course being an attorney's wife would be better than marrying a farmer, she supposed.

Without any distinct wish about it Bessie let a marriage with Thomas be arranged for her. He proposed, and she accepted, since marriage was the lot of girls as everybody she knew looked upon it, and twenty-one was old enough, her father seemed to think, for her to be settling down in life. The day of the acceptance she felt reluctant to have the news broken at once to Kenneth. It seemed a breach of faith with him. Who would take care of his housework now? He shouldn't be out at that ranch all alone, and it would not be right for him to marry just to have a housekeeper, with him only nineteen years old.

When next she saw Kenneth, as he came from his ranch one day, both he and she were uncomfortable. It wasn't as though she could tell him, or even by her attitude to Thomas make Kenneth feel, that she definitely wished to marry Thomas, who seemed a stranger to her yet. Something that others outside her seemed to expect of life was bringing about this marriage, but what could she tell her father? There was no evidence that she would ever love any other man who would come into her life more than she did Thomas, towards whom she felt slightly protective. Perhaps love would come after marriage. But now she felt estranged towards

Kenneth, and he seemed to evade her until one day they were alone together.

"You'll be going away soon Bessie," Kenneth said then. "And Mr. Campbell"—Kenneth never called him Thomas—"tells father he's going to another town to settle after your marriage."

Bessie choked a breath before she could answer. "I don't know Kennie," she said weakly, "It has to be I suppose. Father is so pleased too that one of his daughters should be marrying so well-read a man. He's always been partial to book learning." Bessie stood looking distantly out of the window. Kenneth knew she was controlling tears, and she did not cry easily.

"See here Bessie," he said gruffly, "if you feel like crying about it don't you marry him. We were well enough off at the ranch. Don't let father make you. Even if you angered him I'm started enough now so that I could take care of you."

Bessie wiped her eyes with her hands. "It isn't that Ken. Father wouldn't be one to force me to marry if he thought I didn't want it. You mustn't think that when he's always been just and good. It's only with his religion that he's severe and that's the Scotch of it. You don't understand. We're young now, and you're younger than I, but someday I might be standing in your way, and nobody for me to marry. We must go on with things the way others have before us—and it isn't that I don't want to marry Thomas either. I don't understand what I feel, but just weak and sad at leaving all I've known for strange places, and I'm not knowing what it will be like with him either."

"Don't let any strange places scare you Bessie," Kenneth told her, awkwardly putting his arm about her shoulder. Feeling his affectionate embrace Bessie turned and buried her head on his shoulder unable to control her sobs now. He stroked her hair, as her tears fell upon his neck. Soon her sobs subsided. She placed her hand upon the side of his face.

"There won't be any happier years than the ones I've had with you Kennie; my little brother Kennie; and you're so grown up now," Bessie said, and kissed him. He held her closely for a moment, and then turned quickly and went out of the room. To both of them it seemed impossible that they could control their grief, or ever confront the possibility of this separation that now seemed for all time.

Bessie, remembering that last scene, felt its emotion now, after twenty years, almost as keenly as then, but with a profundity added to the sharpness of its pain, because of what the years had done. Hard farm work after twenty years had made Kenneth into a middle aged and silent man, and he'd never married. With her, there had from the beginning been constant quarrels with Thomas, and attempts on his part when he was in a temper to strike her; and there were the children; continual movings from house to house, or from town to town in an attempt to get decently established. But she must be just to Thomas. Sometimes he was gentle. It was continual money worry, and the number of children about—and the older children were self-willed, as Isabel even advised her mother to leave her husband, and scoffed at marriage, and had none of the respect for religious principles which Bessie believed guided her life.

It was past half past one. The dinner was quite ready and had merely to be kept warm for the guests to arrive before it could be set upon the table. The children were hanging around the kitchen anxiously, sniffing the air, asking Bessie for the turkey gizzard, or heart, or perhaps a taste of dressing. She gave four year old Donnie the gizzard, and seven-year-old Rhoda the liver and did not stop Irene and Harry from sampling the dressing so long as she saw they didn't take too much. She was anxious about John and wished he'd come back, rather than go tramping about the fields brooding till he'd be late for dinner. However bitter he felt about his father he needn't take it out on her, and he was her son as much as his father's, so he should know that his right in the household was good if she wished it, since her father's money helped keep the household going.

There was a knock at the kitchen door, which stood open. Bessie turned to see Farmer Sampson standing there, his usually jovial, sandy-bearded face rather perturbed, almost ashamed looking. She greeted him, telling him to come in, and then saw back of him Farmer Holthausen, his Holland neighbor.

"Good day to you, Mrs. Campbell, a—good day to you," Mr. Sampson said, and halted, and stuttered, then was silent, shifting from one foot to another.

A sharp feeling of terror shot through Bessie as she looked at Mr. Sampson's face. "What is it Mr. Sampson?" she demanded, "You should be at your Thanksgiving dinner at this time."

"Well, Mrs. Campbell, I don't quite know how to tell ye—it's bad news—thar's been an accident—

"Yes," Bessie said sharply, "what is it—John—is it something about John? I didn't want him to go hunting with that gun."

Mr. Sampson did not answer but looked silently at Bessie whose face had gone white and tense. Farmer Holthausen moved clumsily towards her and put out a hand to steady her, afraid that she would faint.

"The boy was climbing over the fence and the gun was cocked and went off," he told her.

"Where is he? Have you brought my boy?"

Farmer Holthausen gestured towards the door, and the three went out, Mr. Sampson with his arm about Bessie's shoulder to steady her. Through eyes before which emotion was spreading a dazzle she saw John seated in a buggy by the gate. He was not dead then, only wounded.

John however was dead. They carried him into the house and laid him upon a couch. She touched his face with her hand. It was cold. His eyes were closed.

Bessie could say nothing. Tears did not come to her eyes. Her husband came into the room and started to speak gruffly, about the dinner, and halted, seeing two men, and then noticed John upon the couch with Bessie standing beside him pale and quiet.

"There will be no Thanksgiving dinner for guests today,

Thomas," Bessie said after a minute, averting her face so as not to look at him. "It is ready. I can not serve it."

Her husband came to her, and said "Well Bessie—" reaching out his hand to put it upon her shoulder. It was trembling. Quickly the perspiration came to his forehead. He could say nothing more. She stood for a moment, then turned and went to the kitchen scarcely aware of the other children who stood silently around, or came and went in silent longing to comfort her.

By three o'clock Bessie had in somewise controlled herself after sitting for a time in her bedroom. Isabel, her seventeen year old daughter, was ready to serve dinner to the family. Mrs. Todd came in to help her, but left, after seeing that John's body was taken to his room to be prepared for burial the next day. So the family sat at the table and ate silently, except that two of the children left quickly when overcome with weeping. Thomas Campbell could eat little and said nothing. Soon he too arose and went to sit in the big arm chair in his library. Bessie came in for a moment. "You had best ask Rev. Jay to preach the burial service, Thomas," she said.

"God's will be done, Bessie," Thomas answered, and could say nothing else. Death left him dumfounded, not quite with grief. He had no great paternal love for his son; he had no great love for Bessie. He had only life, and his questions about himself and life beyond, which frightened him to think of. What affection he might have at moments for his family was only a sympathy of life wonder. There could be no comforting words spoken between him and Bessie, but a fear that beneath her silent grief she felt him blameworthy, was in him.

Three weeks passed. The routine of life continued for Bessie. Children to be fed, prepared for school, their clothes mended, stockings darned, meals cooked; church and prayer meeting to be attended (though she was growing laxer), and calls to be received from people she knew little of who came to offer condolences. Afternoons however some one of the children coming in upon their mother over her work basket, or in the kitchen preparing food, found her crying. She would hastily wipe her tears away, her lips trembling, and would say, if it was one of the older children, "Poor John, and he expected and he wanted so much." Then she would try to dismiss the subject from her mind, as one to talk of.

Isabel came home one afternoon and said "Well, Mother, I start teaching out in the country after Christmas. I passed the exams all right and have a school, so I won't wait to finish the Normal. I can do that later when I have my own money. The Board didn't want to give it to me, saying I was too young, but I persuaded them I could manage."

"O Isabel," Bessie said feebly, feeling the complete disintegration of her family beginning now; "wait until next year, and finish the Normal. The pay is so much better too."

"And live on father who did John to death," Isabel burst forth.

"Isabel, Isabel—your father's temper conquers him, but he was not responsible for that accident."

"Bah! Accident! Don't you suppose I've talked to John about how he felt. He knew how to handle a gun."

Bessie's heart stopped for a moment, and she made no answer because dizziness was upon her. Isabel, seeing her face, felt a pang at having made the remark she had, but quickly, to slip over the idea, she tried to express further indignation at her father. "A lot life is worth living in a household with that old man. I can earn my own living, and maybe I can help you too some, mother."

Had John killed himself? The thought gnawed into Bessie's mind and put into her emotions conflicting currents of fury at, first Thomas, and then at—just fate. After all, it was best that Isabel should go to the country and teach, for her temper would be sure to flame out at her father someday, as her indifference to his remarks now was contemptuous with cold anger, and revolting hatred of his tyranny. Fortunately Thomas did not attempt much to discipline Isabel now, not since last year when he'd threatened to whip her and she had run out of the house to a neighbor's for protection, and told them the story.

January came around and with it the day that Isabel was to

depart for the country, where she would stay at a farm house near the school in which she was to teach.

"I hate leaving," she told Bessie. "You don't know how to handle father. He'll be such a tyrant as never lived with you and the others all afraid of him. But I'd shoot him if he ever tried lifting a hand at me again. Why do you stay with him? You could go to Kentucky and stay with Uncle Kenneth."

"I don't know that Kenneth would be wanting me and my troubles on his hands; and he didn't bring you all into the world to have to care for you."

"What did you let yourself have so many children for? Neither of you wanted us; we're all accidents; and you needn't talk about it being a sin to prevent babies to me. I'm not giving a damn what is or isn't sinful."

"People of my generation weren't so disrespectful of all existing decencies, Isabel."

"Existing decencies! Bah! What are they?—Thank God I'm going away, and can earn my own living now," Isabel said as a last remark, before getting into a buggy to drive into the country. "You won't see me for three weeks anyway; then I might come in for the weekend if I think I can stomach being in the same house with that old devil."

As Isabel drove away Bessie stood at the gateway entrance to the house looking after her. She was strong, and young, and arrogant-willed yet, but so bitter. Tears came to Bessie's eyes, but she pursed her lips in an attempt at determination and went back into the house to take up her work basket. Now and then she put it down to go to the door and call baby Irene so as to know that she was not getting too far from the house, or playing out in the road. She worried little about Irene's childish impishness however, as little danger could come to her in this quiet neighborhood.

She wondered dazedly. Had she been too acquiescent to Thomas' moods and anger. Could she have quelled them with an indignation as hot as Isabel's could be at moments? Well, she hadn't been trained to know how to meet such tempers, and she didn't make the demands on life that her children made, particularly John—before he was gone where he was demanding nothing—and Isabel. She'd been trained to simple desires. Would Isabel be satisfied after she'd worked her way through college? That restlessness in Isabel hadn't come from her.

As Bessie reflected she felt beaten, as never before in her life, and wept weakly, for John—still he might never have been happy as his father never had been. She cried for herself, for Isabel, for the ache of desire to have John alive yet, around so that she could see the beauty of his young body moving about; so that she could feel his young boasting strength beneath which, even when he was sullen, he silently demonstrated a dependence on her. She cried helplessly, for Thomas and his unreasonable temper; she cried simply because of life. Then she straightened herself as she saw Irene coming into her busily to show a young kitten she had discovered and was carrying by the nape of the neck proudly, because she wanted her mother to see that she could carry a kitten rightly. Bessie could not let the baby see her weeping. And she was not the only mother who'd lost a child. Some others had no other children, too. Still the ache was there. Life would go on nevertheless. She petted Irene and told her to run out and play again after giving her bread with butter and sugar. Then she began to get supper. She felt wearily sad about this; because she was not given time for grief that was in her to clarify itself, become sharp in outlines, and remain clearly within her. The ache could only continue, and recur at odd moments. Exhaustion had her spirits, but there were the children to be brought up and somehow given an education that would start them out.

"Things will come out all right," she sighed to herself without conviction. Change of a sort had come within her; Thomas did not baffle her and could not tyrannize over her emotions now, because she didn't care enough to oppose him.

There was no decision for her to make. Life was going on. It would have to solve itself for them all. There was so little more than she had, that she could expect for herself or for the children, through any change or move that she could will to make or imagine.

Professor Granger was damned if there weren't too many young ones around his house, and on his scant salary as a chemistry professor. It was a good thing for him that his wife had refused to move around with him on his various positions at small universities, even if it meant his living alone most of every year.

More than once the professor had insinuated to his wife, known in Wentworth as old Mrs. Granger, and believed the first year or so to be a widow, that some other man than he had had something to do with his family, as it could be seen with half an eye that two or three of the children didn't resemble him in any slight way. He didn't actually believe that, but a household full of youngsters of all ages, raising perdition and bedlam about the house, with not one of them knowing the slightest principle regarding law and order, was enough to tax a man's sense of justice and patience.

Mr. Granger was a small sinewy man, with very grey hair, upon which he used black tea to conceal his age. A ragged goatlike beard decorated his chin, and his dim blue eyes behind powerful glasses peered out at events with a worried look, a look mixed with distrust, hope, and bewilderment. His thin oval face and high thin nose seemed always leading his stooped frame about. For thirty years he'd travelled from town to town, and state to state, with his family, as it seemed impossible for him to retain an instructor's job, as chemistry professor, in any small college for more than a year, or at the most two years. And he wanted to move. Now his family had no longer moved with him for the last five years, and he'd chosen Wentworth as a place to locate them because near it was a farm of 160 acres he had purchased in the years back when farmlands, claims, had sold for almost nothing because of famine years that had struck the community.

Boyle Granger, the youngest of the ten children in the family, watched with his seven-year-old eyes the approach of his father down the lane to their house on the outskirts of town. Prof. Granger had been home for but two days, and Boyle was shy with him. His bent figure moved quickly, as though he were angry about something. His actions were always jerky. Boyle supposed he'd been talking to himself again, and in the doing had whipped himself into a frenzy of fury at the imaginary opponent with whom he argued. Concealing himself around the corner of the house Boyle saw that his supposition had been correct. The old man's face was wrought up, and his pale eyes were flickering lights of angry emotion.

"You're a scoundrel and a ruffian, I tell you. I'll have the law upon you. I'll have you horsewhipped in the public square and run out of town, do you hear me?" Boyle heard his father saying, as he stood on the porch to hurl defiance at his unseen opponent before going into the house. Boyle wondered who it was the old man imagined he was addressing now. Was it brother Jim, or someone in the family? He however was afraid to go inside the house where his father was, because a dread of being alone with his father when he was talking to himself possessed him.

When Boyle did go into the house a half hour later he found his mother and father quarreling furiously.

"You're an ignorant hill woman, nothing more," Mr. Granger hurled out at his wife, his whole small body tightened up with nervous fury. "A negligent slut who has brought the curse of indolence to all the household. There isn't a trace of moral stamina in any of the blood flowing within you, or your children."

"Have done with your abuses and go to your room, or go out of the house," old Mrs. Granger answered him, looking for the time being not at all the harried old lady she often appeared. "I have no need to be listening to your tirades; you may go back to your school and stay there, if you have not, as of course you have, lost that position through your godless temper."

Boyle crept through the room and ran upstairs where he remained until the clamour downstairs made him aware that dinner was ready. The quarrel between his parents had subsided as Boyle knew it would have by the time the older children came home.

"Father is going out to his farm to stay a few days," Mrs. Granger informed them at the dinner table. "He won't want being alone out there, but it wouldn't do to take any of you older children away from your studies, so I suppose Boyle had better go along with his father."

"We'll get on capitally together," Mr. Granger said in a conciliatory manner to Boyle. "We'll be all cozy, and hunky dory out there, with that woodstove, and the food we can cook together. It will teach you self-dependence too."

Boyle looked sulky, but was afraid to express the distaste he had for going out to the farm alone with his father, though he had slight realization of what it would be like. The summer previous he'd been at the farm which lay sixteen miles from Wentworth, but with him then had been the whole family. Grain fields had stretched from the farm house to the horizon, except for a few occasional cut-ins by country roads. All that summer had been a driftingly happy one for him, one lighted by clear days of warmth, and carefree playing amongst stretches of woods down the road always, with his brothers and sisters to take him for walks of miles, to swim, or to visit farm neighbors. There had been bird nests to explore; the kingbirds to watch growing up in their nest built in the old up-turned plow; swallows too, which had nested in the eaves of the barn and house. But winter there? Boyle thought he must do something to get out of going with his father. He wouldn't know how to act, or what to say to the old man.

"What's papa going out to the farm for?" Boyle asked his mother out in the kitchen after dinner.

"Another renter has gone back on him, and he has to go out and see that all the granaries are locked up, and the stables, so that marauders won't take away what little farm machinery there is. He thinks too he can manage to sell the farm as we are needing the money to live on."

With a sense of bleakness Boyle heard the answer. He wondered what would happen to them all if his father sold the farm and then spent the money he got from it. They'd have nothing, he knew from what his mother often said.

"But I don't want to go with him, mamma. He talks to himself, and he'll be cranky all the time when we're alone."

"You must learn to put up with a few things Boyle," his mother said. "I would rather you did not go, but there is no knowing what would become of him out there alone in his state of mind. You'll be company, and he is different with you than he has ever been with the older children. You haven't had nearly so much discipline. The Schrader farm is only two miles away and you certainly haven't forgotten how to walk down two miles of road. One of the girls certainly can't go with him, and with the older boys it would be one continual battle."

The next morning Boyle ran from his cold room upstairs to dress in front of the hard coal stove. Through the isinglass a red glow shone. He took off his nightdress and stood naked before the redhot stove so that he'd quickly have the chill out of him. By the time he'd had his porridge his father was at the house with a team of horses he'd hired for several days from the Livery Stable. A few bags of provisions were piled into the back of the carriage, and the two drove off. His father seemed in great good humour today, and gave Boyle a nickel to buy candy with, so that Boyle didn't for a moment think to dread the week to be spent alone with his father as he had the night before. He had an instinct that the old man knew that he wasn't so afraid of his father, as he was inclined to dislike and pity him a little; and so his father tried to pamper him.

The first night of their arrival Boyle was tired with the long drive in the cold, through which he'd been huddled up under a fur robe most of the time, tiring his back and neck. At four o'clock in the afternoon they arrived at the Schrader's farm and arranged to have a hot dinner there at six o'clock before going on to the farm. In consequence of the hot meal and another two mile drive in the cold after dinner, Boyle could barely keep his eyes open by the time they arrived at the farmhouse. In ten minutes he was curled up on the floor near the woodstove fire, and sleeping on top of and under a number of blankets, most of them musty smelling as they'd been left in the deserted farmhouse for some months.

The next morning, after eating pancakes his father made out of patent flour-batter fried on the woodstove, Boyle ran outdoors to explore buildings he'd known in the summer months. In the barn where there had been two cows and a horse during that period, there was now nothing but frosted manure upon the earthen floor, and an odour of staleness. The desolation of the barn chilled him. The old turned up plow off to the side of the barn was rustier than ever; the kingbird's nest was shattered by the wind; looking in every direction he saw only bare stubble fields upon which lay a light covering of dirty snow that had lain for weeks. As he wondered if he dared try to run over to Fader's farm, more than two miles crisscross his father's land, he felt no wish to do so. Mrs. Fader would be cross with him maybe, as she, a hunchback, often was, and certainly would be in this desolate season and surroundings. He did not know what to do with himself. There was not even any work his father could set him to as he could not chop wood with the big axe his father had brought along. It was too heavy.

With delight, after lunch, he noticed that it was snowing lightly. All the mildly cold blue air was filled with a dazzle of snowflakes falling, swirling and being blown by a faint wind. Outside he went to make a snow man, and to see the shapes of snowflakes on his dark overcoat. Within a half an hour the ground, as far as his eyes could see, was clean white, since enough snow had fallen to cover all the dirt-crusted snow of weeks back.

As day lengthened into night the snow fell heavier, constantly heavier, and the wind came mightily from the north. Prof. Granger had seen to it that plenty of wood to keep a fire for several days had been cut and brought into the house. Boyle felt strangely removed from everything in the world; from himself even; as though he weren't in his body or that his body wasn't his. There was nothing about to connect him with things he knew of. There was nothing about to feel or think of. And he could only answer his father's questions since he had no wish to consult his father on anything. His father was just an old man that he couldn't pretend to understand or know what he'd do next. There was the sky, darkening with night; the snow-covered prairies which looked all level, and the same, as far as he could see them through the falling greyness of snow in night's oncoming darkness.

At eight o'clock, when he should have been sleepy, Boyle was more wakeful than he thought he had ever been before in his life; and not wakeful with curiosity or desire to do anything, or even to tell himself stories. No stories would come. He was just wakeful with a dumbness and numbness of consciousness of all the space surrounding him. The wind outside had become a gale; the soft white snow was no longer falling. In its place an angry steel-ice sleet was whipping and cutting through the air, beating against the walls of the farmhouse through which cold came in gusts, full blast, so that the brightly burning woodstove seemed to have no power to conquer the coldness of them. It was as though the stove sat out in the open prairie trying to warm all the universe of outdoors.

"Well Boyle, it looks like we're in for a blizzard," Prof. Granger said, wanting to break the silence. "That may mean a siege of several days but we're supplied with food, and enough coal so we can manage if the wood runs out."

Boyle sat up in bed. His blue eyes were feverishly large, and luminous, and his straw hair was rumpled. If it had been somebody else other than his father he'd have wanted to crawl into bed with him for the company of a body. All he did however was to answer "yes," to his father.

The noise of the gale seemed to increase in momentum, like something winding, winding, winding, and rising to a higher shriek continually without ever breaking into a torrent of shrieks. Thousands of cats might have been snarling in fury at the night;

babies wailing; dogs moaning; women crying out. A still dread that had incomprehensible presentiments within it kept Boyle quiet; he had no terror; only a stillness of dread, benumbed.

Ten o'clock approached, and gradually Boyle curled into his pile of blankets and went to sleep. He would have slept till morning, but a cry from his father awoke him. He lay still

His father had jumped out of bed and was pacing and fuming about the room storming at some imaginary person. He would whirl suddenly as though to confront and give battle to this person. Boyle was quiet in his blankets, wishing he had courage to speak to his father, and remind him that someone was hearing him talk to himself, which he denied doing. He knew if he spoke that would stop his father for a few minutes, and maybe let Boyle go to sleep again.

"There's not a trace of moral conviction in your nature; you're rotten, soul and body, I say to you," Prof. Granger was saying in tones trembling with a passion of fury and eloquence. "You're damned to everlasting hellfires and perdition, where lowlived scoundrels such as yourself belong." He turned with a sudden rage, and seemed to be ready to pounce in Boyle's direction. Perhaps his father was mad, as older brother Jim suggested at times. Boyle knew he had to speak.

"O papa, you waked me up by talking aloud to yourself. There isn't anybody here but me," he finally spoke trying to keep any fear out of his voice.

"What's that? What's that? O Boyle," his father answered, turning quickly at the sound of a voice "Tush, what is this? You should be sleeping sound as a tick, hours ago. Off to sleep with you."

Boyle felt easier within himself now that his father was talking to him, and ventured to say "but I can't sleep if you jump around the room, jarring the floor, can I?"

"Off to sleep with you. You should be snoozing warm as a cricket in a rug by now. No more of your nonsense," Prof. Granger said, getting under his own covers.

Boyle cuddled under the covers again and was soon off to sleep, which was not interrupted until seven o'clock in the morning, though dreams and nightmares came to him, some of which seemed but continuations of reality and conversations that had taken place in his waking states of consciousness.

In the morning Boyle again awoke because of a shout from his father. He was drowsy-eyed the first minute, and rubbed his eyes.

"There's a white wolf out by the barn," his father exclaimed excitedly as though frightened. Boyle jumped out of his covers and ran to the window. "There'll be a pack of those great grey timber wolves surrounding us," the old man added. Boyle could see against the whiteness of the snow, that having fallen steadily for over fifteen hours had by now covered all the landscape with a three or four feet depth of snow.

"It's running across the snow; it heard me shout," his father explained, "see, see, there," as he pointed out across the snow.

Boyle's still sleep-dulled eyes could not be sure whether they discerned a wolfish white figure gliding across the snow or not. The light was beginning to appear dimly through the dawn-dullness so that a faint dazzle was in the air.

His father quieted down. Boyle dressed, and while waiting for his breakfast, which his father was cooking upon the stove, he went to stand looking out of the window, wondering if there had surely been a white wolf, as he remembered, brother Jim said that father was always imagining packs of grey timber wolves were around the country, when few had been seen about for five years or more.

Looking from the window he saw the long stretch of white snow, level in stretches, and again swirled into snowbanks by the hurricane that had swept the country last night. Some of the banks must have been twelve feet high. The snow went on, on, white, and glistening, until with a sharper definition it cut into the horizon. It was as though the sky were a great bowlike mouth that was swallowing all the clear snow landscape, as the whiteness of the snow had swallowed the white wolf, if there had been a white wolf. Boyle wondered. The snow would take him into itself too if he were to run far, far out into it; the snow and the distance, but he knew he didn't dare go out into it now because he'd be buried in some drift away from the house, probably if he tried walking. That cut him completely off from everybody. No matter what happened, or however much he might want to run to the Fader farm, or to the Schraders, he could not, because even the roads were concealed and he'd lose his way were he able to plod through the soft snow.

"We're in for a siege," his father said. "We should not have sent those horses back to be stabled at the Schrader farm, and then I could have driven to their place."

"We can walk to their farm can't we?"

"I'd have to be carrying you through the snow banks, and the snow is deep enough to bury me too."

But before noon Boyle saw some horses coming towards the house from the direction of Schraders'. It was Mr. Schrader and a son, come to find out how they were, and soon they were in the house. Mr. Schrader talked jovially to Boyle about the great warm dinner he'd be having within an hour at their farmhouse.

"That'll keep the health in those cheeks of yours, though they're as fat as red apples now," he said, pinching Boyle's cheek.

Soon the whole lot of them were in the buggy and on their way to the Schrader farm. It made Boyle feel warm and cozy inside to think of being there, in the big kitchen near the cooking stove, and there'd be the two cats, and the big sheepdog in the house too. Thinking about these things he snuggled back into his heavy overcoat and against the fur robes.

"Can I have a big bowlful of fresh milk to drink too," he asked Mr. Schrader, "just fresh from the cow."

"But sonny, we only milk in the morning and in the evening, so you can't have fresh warm milk this time, as your father says he'll drive back to town after dinner. You can have all of the morning milk you want though."

Boyle cuddled against Mr. Schrader's knee, and contented himself with anticipating how comfortable it would be in the Schrader kitchen playing with the cats, the sheepdog, and the Schrader children.

After the departure of Mrs. Daly from Wentworth there was some difficulty in getting a librarian who could keep the books in order at the Public Library. Where she had kept fairly up to date about popular, and more or less good class books, old Miss Waters, who was substitute librarian, did nothing. She was simply a poverty-stricken woman of some fifty years of age, who for the last twenty-five years at least, if not for all her life, had been simply dazed by circumstances which encompassed her existence. Nevertheless, inadequate as she was, she had to suffice as the salary was not sufficient to attract a woman of greater abilities.

Such being the case, when Father Flynn, president of the Library board, received a letter from Phyllis Pond, he thought that reports about her having become more sensible since she'd left Wentworth might be believed sufficiently to give her a trial as librarian.

Eight years before this time Phyllis Pond was a noisy little town girl with a snub nose, impish eyes, an impertinent manner, and very ordinary looks that were not added to by her inclination to be dirty through romping into boys' games, baseball in the summer, snowball fights in the winter, and kid combats all the year around. The summer of her fifteenth year however she went away with her father who owned a merry-go-round which he took to county fairs, village carnivals, and to larger villages before or after circus performances. She spent the summer taking up tickets on the merry-go-round for him, and when she returned in the fall, she was a painted beauty; plucked her eyebrows, carmined her lips, rouged, and went in for fancy coiffeurs. It was thought too that she took some preparation to give pallor to her skin. During the three years' time that she remained in town no definite scandal circulated about her, as she did not meet trains coming into town, and was not known to be about much with young men, but she was too friendly with Mrs. Watkins who had been her schoolteacher in the country some years back.

When Phyllis left Wentworth in her seventeenth year she had a reputation of being fast, of putting on too many grand manners for a girl of so common a family, and of being impudent to all her instructors at the Normal School, though it was not denied that she had a mind and achieved good marks with little effort. At the State University to which she went, people heard, she was popular with her fellow students, made a good sorority, and graduated with honors. Mrs. Hammer of the W.C.T.U., who had encountered her out of town, declared that anyone would be surprised at the change in her manner. She used make-up no longer, and while a pretty girl without it, was quiet and ladylike in her demeanor.

It was a great error then, which she made upon returning to Wentworth with the chance of becoming librarian, when she went to stay for the first week with Mrs. Watkins. Of course she probably did not know what Mrs. Watkins had become in the years of her absence, but she must have known what the older woman had always been suspected of.

Before her marriage to Tom Watkins, Florine Watkins had been a schoolteacher in the country. A vivid colouring of face, great dark eyes, coarse black hair, and full over-red lips, made her then a striking though not a beautiful figure. Even in those years it was supposed she had kept older farmboys in her school after hours for no decent purpose, and it was a shock to Tom's family when he married her, though he was dissipated himself, and had, instead of going into the grain business with his father, become a railroad engineer as many another young man about the community had done.

The first year of their marriage, Tom took to drinking harder than ever before; while Florine was known to be much too friendly with men stopping off at the two hotels in town. Whatever scenes there were between Tom and Florine, she had him bested in the way of a flaming temper, and drove him from the house several times with an assault of dishes. He would stay away for weeks at a time, but he always, for the first ten years came back, and by now there were five children, two of them twins. All of the children except Lucile, the eldest, who looked like Florine, resembled the Watkins family, and it looked as if Ellen, the second girl, would be just such a Christian-Endeavor, Sunday-School-going old maid as her aunt of the same name; weazened, tight-faced, prim, and disapproving of many things. The older Watkins wanted to adopt her, and she was ready; Lucile however cherished a resentment against her father's family, believing that they'd never done what they might have to make Tom help support his family rather than leaving it all on Florine's hands.

By the time Phyllis Pond returned Mrs. Watkins was quite openly keeping a free house for young bloods of the town; and even twelve-year-old Lucile appeared to be slated for a bad career, which was a shame, because doubtlessly it was only her awareness of what her mother stood for that made her cut up out of abandon. Within the last year she'd chosen to forsake playing with children of better families, and was about with younger Crawshaw and Ford girls.

Phyllis Pond arrived, and as she went down the main street of the town nobody recognized her, but instead wondered who the good looking girl in a white broadcloth suit was; and when two days later it was known to be Phyllis and that she was staying with Mrs. Watkins, people wondered. Was she going Mrs. Watkins' way? She stayed in town for about a month, and was seen seldom on the streets, and when she did appear, she came and went unobtrusively, making no attempt to re-acquaint herself with anybody. But her chance of being librarian was of course gone. When she departed it was discovered that her father had died, leaving no money, so that her stay with Mrs. Watkins had been a more or less enforced one as she was friendly with no one else in town, and had little money after finishing college. During her stay in town she had managed to secure a position as teacher in a town some distance from Wentworth.

Not until five years later was Phyllis Pond heard of again, and then she came to town, the wife of a well to do lumber merchant in South Dakota. Her husband was sufficiently well off, and connected with business interests in town through a chain lumber concern, so that Phyllis was re-instated in the good graces of the town populace, and her past was commented on as a mixture of indiscretion, and ignorance of Mrs. Watkins' true character. Anyway, by this time, Mrs. Watkins' suicide was a three year old fact. In the note which Florine had left she wrote that after fifteen years of trying to support her children on her husband's drinking habit, she'd decided it wasn't worth while, and the children would have to be taken care of as time other than her own dictated. Accordingly the older Watkins took over the children and attempted to instill into them Christian Presbyterian ideas and habits; but Lucile at sixteen disappeared, and it was only some months after her disappearance that it became known she'd married a fifty year old auctioneer and dealer in horses, about whom there had been considerable scandal.

It was at about this time too that the Haroldson family so suddenly disintegrated. Michael Haroldson was part owner of the Haroldson Mill. He was a quiet, worn-looking man of forty years, and his flagrant, blond wife seemed contented enough as they had one of the finest houses in town, and three children whom a mother could be proud of. And her husband gave her complete use of the family automobile, and would have gladly permitted her to do all of the entertaining she wished had she shown any inclination to do so. She however had to take frequent trips out of town, leaving her husband and the children to be taken care of by a housekeeper who conducted the household. One time she did not return, but instead wrote back saying she had gone away with the chauffeur—the only chauffeur employed by a private family in town. Her destination was California.

Mr. Haroldson put his two fourteen-year-old daughters into a Catholic seminary so that they would have careful instruction; his boy he sent to a military school; and his house he rented out at a miserably low rent to old Mrs. Granger, whose husband had again departed to a position in a high school, this time, rather than a college. Soon he was gone from town also, and two years later died, leaving little enough money so that the children would have to shift for themselves.

Migration from Wentworth now was taking place at a great rate; old Mrs. Mc Pherson moved to Long Beach, California; soon after her step-son-in-law and family followed. The Toppens moved to Sioux City, Iowa; Mrs. Hammer, since prohibition had come to the town, was no longer able to keep interested in W.C.T.U. work, and moreover, her husband's grain elevator business had lost a great deal of money through mis-investments. They too left town, going to Detroit, Michigan, and the oldest son Percy, had to leave college in his second year to become a wage earner as an office man of some sort. With the Reeves, the Jenkins, the Reynalds, and the Freeman families all gone from town, Gene Collins returning on his second leave from West Point, found scarcely one of his old friends and schoolmates left for him to chum with and talk over old times during his two weeks' stay in town. The Downing girls were away teaching physical culture and would not come back for the summer vacations except every other year; Mary Warden lived in Minneapolis, or travelled in Europe. Even Alberta Kingston no longer met the trains to encounter travelling salesmen; now at thirty, she had consented to marry a young farmer.

Mrs. Bell's boarding house now comprised two buildings, and her younger daughter, Lela, who people had thought would make a name for herself as a musician with her remarkable ability as pianist, was playing in the town moving-picture house, and she was being as careless about the men she consorted with as any girl of good family had ever been, and once she'd been more critical of indiscretion than either the Fitzgerald or Warden girls. So Gene Collins was hard put to it to amuse himself for two weeks, and, because he knew he would be assigned to Washington for a time after finishing West Point or that at least he would not be back in Wentworth for some years, he found that Daisy La Brec, of a family formerly despised, was as amusing a companion as any other girl about town, unless he wanted to be around with girls of from fifteen to nineteen years of age; and at twenty four he wasn't old enough not to want girls more of his own time, as his was a serious, ambitious nature.

Probably it was because the economic conditions of the country about had once made it a paying thing to have large families that there existed both in Wentworth, the towns adjacent, and in the county, so many families of great size. In Larkville, a town of but three hundred inhabitants, situated ten miles from Wentworth, there was the Rosen family, which numbered in its elder branch fifteen children. All of them were grown up and most of them were married and parents of families of their own. In Larkville the bank was owned by a Rosen son-in-law; the mill and elevator by a Rosen son, and a Rosen son-in-law respectively; and the big grocery store that served all the farm community was owned by another Rosen son. So that sheerly by size of family the Rosens virtually owned and controlled all of the business and production of the village and farm community about them. Thus they were able to aid each other in accumulating wealth.

Around Wentworth there were five farmer families almost of a size equal to the Rosen family. The Macalasters, less mercenary and practical, had still managed to make good fortunes for themselves, and had also become acceptable to the townspeople as equals. The Macalasters were a generous-hearted, hospitable family, and liked much entertaining at their homestead farm, with country dances and other parties at which vast quantities of food were served. But with this generation the popularity of the large family had died away. It was coming to be thought hardly respectable to have families of more than four, or six at the most. This had something to do perhaps with the number of indigent, almost pauperish, great-sized families about in the community, for unless the members of big families were hard working, and ready to co-operate with each other in their efforts, a big family was in no way advantageous.

There was the Ellis family; a goodnatured, quick-tempered, irresponsible, French-Irish family, who had not in twenty years managed to stay more than three years on any one farm. They were always renters. Their pigs were allowed to run about in the back-yard of the lots surrounding the farmhouse. Crops were late in being planted, and let to stand too long before being harvested. Mrs. Ellis, an amazingly vivacious and energetic woman of fifty, managed to make money off her butter and eggs, and tried to keep her husband and sons keyed up to getting their work done on time. But both the Ellis boys and girls were given to traipsing about the country, beauing away, giggling, coquetting, and wanting to ar-range dances and parties wherever they saw the slightest chance. Three of the Ellis boys had married. Pat Ellis had his own farm now, a small place with a tiny shack, in which his pretty peas-antlike, blond wife worked potteringly, while Pat slouched about, feeding the hogs, doing a little farm work, but fiddling away most of the time at an old violin, while cursing his hired man for not getting all of the work done as he'd been directed. As a school-teacher of the country school near his shack was reported to be game, and more than game for humping, Pat's younger brothers drove to his farm eight miles from their own, frequently. And the schoolteacher was generally around, and ready to take a stroll down the country road with one of them.

Olive Ellis had managed to marry the son of rich old man Baker, a banker in a tiny farm village fifteen miles from their farm. One of the three other Ellis girls had married too, but of course Daisy, a trifle silly—one wouldn't want to say she was an idiot, because Daisy wept very easily—Daisy could hardly be expected to marry, and when the old people were gone some of her brothers or sisters would just have to see that Daisy was taken care of, because she could help about the housework and not be more slovenly about it, heaven knows, than her brothers and sisters were slovenly in their habits, Mrs. Ellis believed, though she wasn't going to complain of the children God had given her.

Something decidedly wrong was up with Fern Ellis, that her mother didn't quite understand, though she suspected—and wasn't going to talk about her suspicion. Fern was thin, dark, hard-bodied, with keen burning brown eyes. She wasn't a girl that men took to much, and a year before had decided she would become a stenographer. Off she went to Sioux Falls and began to take a course at the commercial college there. Before she'd gone there Fern had been a very healthy, lively girl, with any amount of get up and go in her. She hadn't been there for three months before she was taken ill, and was in the hospital for two weeks, though she didn't let any of the family know about it until it was over, and then she said appendicitis, and she needed money to pay for her operation. Within six weeks she was back home and her spirit was broken. She went about dazedly, dull-eyed, and could be interested in nothing. Really she was less to be depended upon than Daisy now. One would think the girl was dying on her feet. It was only when one of her brothers swore at her in a temper that she could flare up with great indignation at the way menfolk thought they could make a slave out of a woman. But they weren't going to treat her that way as she was only their sister, not their wife. But she subsided soon from these flare-ups, and became quieter and quieter. It was evident that she'd catch no man to marry her as she was now. Mrs. Ellis told her daughter-in-law who lived with them—having eloped with nineteen year old Dan Ellis when she discovered she was with child—that she should be very careful and not have any more children for some years. Big families may have been all right at one time but they were too hard to look after in this generation.

In spite of their troubles, however, the Ellis family got on somehow, retained a degree of pride and spirit, and the boys were always game to go hunting with young men from the town. They were a good-hearted, likeable family, quick to temper, quick to forget, irresponsible, but always ready to extend hospitality to anybody they liked. They liked when they liked, and didn't hesitate to let it be known when they disliked.

Chautauqua season was on again, and this year it was to be quite a gay season, as Lake Borrows, which unaccountably for five years had been little more than a swamp, had filled up within the last two years, so that swimming, canoeing, and motorboating were again possible upon it; and in the spring of this year it had been restocked with fish so that within a couple of years fishing from it would again be possible.

Cottages that had not been occupied for seasons were carpentered into shape for a two weeks' camping residence; new shacks were being erected all the late spring, so that now a whole row of resort cottages made a street down what had formerly been called lover's lane. The woods surrounding the lake and cottages extended for miles; along the beach far off from the cottage district, blue cranes, kingfishers, wild ducks and geese, and other birds which had for seasons past deserted the lake, were seen and heard again. The cry of a loon sounded at nighttime, silly laughter the sound. Golden-breasted orioles, kingbirds, cardinals, goldfinches, and innumerable turtle doves, infested the forest as always. Across the lake since the refilling of its basin a small "fish village" had sprung up, though the so-called village consisted of but one shack and a tiny store which intended making its living off young people who rowed across the lake from the Chautauqua grounds. They would want soft drinks, since no other could be had except illicitly. Hot dogs, chocolate, peanuts, and popcorn, would be quite saleable to people after a two-mile row. In this village too were the fish breeding tanks attended to by an old Bohemian who, it was whispered, kept a stock of drinks somewhat harder than pop or cider.

Because of the rumour of what a gay season it would be at the Chautauqua lake this summer, many inhabitants of the younger generation, living out of town now, were supposed to be coming back for vacation periods. Along the row of thirty cottages erected down lover's lane were places of the Degens; the Downings; the Thompsons; the Fitzgeralds; Helaine Blair Conniston; the Scotts; the Coltons; and other families. It was understood that Gladys and Fritzie Hammer were coming to visit Carrie Colton; that Sammy Hardcutt, and Allen Jenkins would be back, the former on a summer's hoboing trip to take in the harvest fields later in the season, the latter to visit Lloyd Scott. It was quite probable too that a number of other old time young people would show up out of curiosity to see what changes were taking place in the old town.

As Lake Borrows was but four miles from Wentworth most of the business and professional men commuted daily; in fact many of them chose to spend their nights in their town houses, and only came out for the weekends after the first two days, when the noises made by the young generation assured them that they would get no extra sleep or vacation rest here. This arrangement was as the young people would have had it, as it permitted them to stay up later nights on swimming, canoeing, dancing, and loving parties. Couples could be seen strolling into the woods until four or five in the morning; the strumming of mandolins, ukeleles, and the whine of sentimental violins sounded across the waters till far into the morning light, while snatches of love songs, comedy ditties and bits of carefree conversation drifted through the forests and across the lake continually. Every night there was a dance in the old dining room of the hotel, in which a piano had been placed, so that when the orchestra was not there, some young person offered to play dance music. Generally it was Genevieve Rich who played, because she was not particularly keen on dancing, as she was supposedly infatuated with the football player, Lenard Colbridge, who paid little attention to her.

Through the two weeks, figures floated past the eyes of the onlooker with a quality of fresh young beauty, irresponsibility, and colouring that was a revelation to an older generation. Young people not of the town had also come to stay at the hotel, or to visit relatives who were of the town. Girls of fourteen, fifteen, and sixteen, who had been unnoticed, awkward, or shy, began to come forth as young ladies vieing with each other and with older girls in ways of dancing, prattling entertainingly, giggling, loving, and presenting beauty, or charm. Boys of all ages found themselves at first confused as to which girl or girls to admire most, though in the end the youngest comers won by the shock of their sudden birth into womanhood, and by their young joyfulness of expectancy. The older girls, read-books as they were, served only for serious conversation, of which there was little. Lenore Thompson was still by age and temperament sure of several seasons' attention however; and Eva Downing claimed a share, because day and night she was irrepressible in her efforts to entertain herself. Till the latest hour her gay contralto voice sounded along the cottage row as she sang, danced solo dances on the grass, and played the carefree good fellow and open-housed hostess to every man about, thus making the Downing cottage a sure rendezvous when the older people in other cottages became austere. She it was who engineered a bar-becue; picnics to be held across the lake; extra dances; and an amateur vaudeville stunt night.

On another lane were a few cottages in which stayed girls from smaller towns surrounding Wentworth, and girls of a class deemed second rate. To these the young men went more or less surrep-titiously, and the young men were disposed to be sheepish if seen by girls of their own set in the company of these others. Several young men had tents together, and late nights, or early mornings, as everybody else in camp was sleeping, to these tents would come groups of young men to talk of their success with the ladies, describing sometimes to what extent any particular girl would permit a man to go in his fondling of her. The slight feeling of restraint in telling about girls deemed of their set was down as regards girls deemed to be strangers; it was down as regards the girls of their set also if the young men gathered together had been intimately acquainted long enough, except when marriage was contemplated.

Lloyd Scott, Allen Jenkins, and Sammy Hardcutt had a tent to themselves, properly, though not a night passed in which Peter

Reynalds, Clarence Potten, or some other young man around twenty wasn't sleeping on the ground inside the tent with them, because of having stayed up too late, loving, or drinking; or because they had no other place to stay in unless they went back to town. All of this lot had been away at college in Wisconsin, at the State University, or at Minnesota. Occasionally the first few nights Gene Collins drifted in, but the others did not like him, and his presence always placed a pall on conversation; they thought he was too West Point-y, and wanted to talk too much of his athletic renown. Glenn Warden and Don Reeves also came to the tent sometimes, as they discovered more sympathy with the young men in this tent than with their former schoolmates of the four year older generation.

A newcomer to town also came into the group. He was known only by the name of Tennessee, and was from Kentucky, in Wentworth visiting a childless uncle and aunt. It was understood that his father and mother had been divorced for some years, and that his trip to North Dakota was simply a hoboing venture with him. He was a dark-skinned, gentle-mannered individual, and was immediately taken up by everybody, much to Lloyd Scott's sorrow in the case of Lenore Thompson, because Lloyd cherished a deep rooted admiration for that young lady, but she was letting Tennessee occupy all her spare time. However Lloyd consoled himself with the fact that Tennessee would be gone after the summer, and then his own chances with Lenore would re-instate themselves

Coming in one night about twelve o'clock a quiet night— Tennessee began to talk at once about his fondness for Lenore.

"Ah'm tellin' you boys, that little lady shuah has me going. Ah's right down fond of her."

"Is she good loving, Ten?" Allen Jenkins asked, not aware of Ten's chivalric attitude and quick temper.

"Well now son," Tennessee drawled, with a darkly southern look upon his face, "ah's not carin' for that little lady foah that sort of thing. She doesn't mind caresses, but theh's no getting too close to her without she wants it. And ah wants to remark she means quite something to me, and you'all not speak too familiah of her if you'all don't mind."

Petei Reynalds stepped into the breach, as he knew Allen hadn't meant the remark slightingly. Allen was simply a blundering dub. "You've luck anyway Ten. That's the way with you Southern guys. Lenore's fallen hard for you, we all can see that, and we all have been admiring her from the distance for some time."

"Hard luck Pete and I had tonight though," Sam Hardcutt cut in. "We sat in the auditorium talking after the concert, and a couple of girls from Dub Row came along. They picked up all right, and went just far enough to get a fellow hot, and then tried to make a date for tomorrow night. That wasn't what we wanted. They were probably a couple of waitresses or farm hicks, to judge from the way they acted, but they weren't having anything this evening."

"Shuah," Tennessee said, "it's them two that live on the edge of the camp I guess. A blond with kinky hair, one of them. Theah fawthah's a rich farmer, but theah's nothing doin' theah, though one of them tries to make you'all think theah is if you'all stick around long enough. Ah tried them one night, though ah wouldn't want Lenore to know about it."

Frenchy, a Canadian boy who had bummed about the world for some years as sailor and flunkey, and who had struck the camp to be clerk at the hotel, peered into the tent and then entered. He had with him a bottle of whiskey a hotel guest had given him as a tip; so all of the young men took a sip. Their voices sounding for some distance brought several other boys and young men to the tent, and soon more drink was located, so that it was seven o'clock in the morning before the party broke up, though some of the men had already stretched themselves on the grassy soil inside or just outside of the tent, and as the night air was balmy, slept.

Two days later was the 4th of July, and there was to be swimming, canoeing and diving contests, as well as various races, 100 yard dashes, three-legged races, barrel and potato races, etc.

It was the great day. By ten o'clock multitudes of people had already congregated, and all the women, particularly, were in festive garb. Bright-coloured blazers, and white trousers decorated a good share of the men also. A sharp wind was up, which fluttered amongst the gay-coloured, or white frocks of the women, revealing the outlines of their figures, and a greater portion of their legs than they pretended to care having revealed. This naturally was occasion for much joking on the part of men about, many of whom seated themselves on the veranda of the hotel to watch the caprices of the wind. To the front of the hotel was a small bluff which stood clear in the sunlight; at one moment when Lela Bell, extremely lithe and slender, appeared on its summit, and stood consciously unconscious while the wind blew around her, the contours of her slim body showed as clearly through her light summer dress as if it had been chiffon and she had on no other garment. When told of this she laughed, and said "Wait till this afternoon; my bathing suit is much less than this dress as a covering. I'd like to shock some of the damned old hens, male and female, about this burg. They talk their heads off about a girl whether she does anything or not, though they are not consulted as guides to behaviour."

Rose Borrows had come to the lake. Her once brawny, bronze-skinned, rich brown-eyed beauty, had softened with marriage and maternity. As she stood talking with Helaine Blair Conniston, it could be noted how her looks had improved, while those of Helaine had nearly disappeared with marriage and the assumption of a matronly appearance. Naomi Morris, who had also come to town after a three-year absence, had improved much in looks with marriage. Formerly she'd been grave, with too hard an outline to her Grecian features, but now she had softened, and her pallor had a luminousness, and her eyes a glow, and her manner a sympathy rather than a reserve, so that it could be seen absence from Wentworth, and marriage to an ex-barber, had been no hardship upon her. And her babies were beautiful, like miniature Chinese emperors that looked out on the world with astounded but curious dark eyes.

Gladys and Fritzie Hammer, visiting Carrie Colton, were in for much attention that was not detracted from, even by the sudden discovery of Blanche Watkins, aged 14, Liz Granger, and Sally Hardcutt, each aged 16, as young ladies, of beauty or gaiety that made them lovable. The point was that all of the young men in camp had decided it was little use concentrating on any girl this season, and so every girl, newly discovered as a belle, was sure that she had captured the favour of several young men, for within six hours of dancing it was possible to have danced several times with several men, and also to have strolled down to the lake to hold confidential conversation with them while watching the moonlight ripple over the waters.

It was commented upon that Don Reeves, married to a rich girl, had not brought his wife with him. So long as he danced and talked with Rose Borrows, Helaine Blair, Naomi Morris or Mary Warden, that could pass as for old times' sake. But the last day or so he had been about much with sixteen-year-old Sally Hardcutt, who seemed to like the idea that she was attracting a married man eight years older than herself. This night she was sitting down on the pier with Don, and was telling him how awfully dull she thought this old tank town was, and how she wanted to go to Vassar, or Wells, or at least to some decent college rather than to these burgish western universities.

"And I think I can get into the ——— sorority, because I have a cousin who belongs to one. That will be much nicer too, because a girl doesn't have any fun at college if she doesn't get in with the right people, does she?"

"But you mustn't say you want to make a sorority, and particularly any special one, because if you were heard to say that on a college campus it might keep you out," Don Reeves advised her. "It's all right to say to me because I understand; and I know how it is. My wife is a ———. She might help you there, but don't say I've told you that."

"She wouldn't like your talking to me like this, would she? Of course she wouldn't be jealous—but why didn't you bring her along?"

"And miss having this chance to get to know you? But—she didn't want to come. She's visiting her family."

"I do wonder where I will go. I just hope I don't have to go to the Normal and take the teacher's course. I'd just hate being a school teacher, after I've always cut up so in school myself too."

Don was sitting very close to Sally. He hadn't intended to put his arm about her, reasoning that that wouldn't be right since she was such a kid. But somehow his arm touched hers, and then it was about her, first because she was sitting so near the edge of the pier and might fall into the water. But once drawing her further back upon the pier his arm stayed about her very gently. Sally felt perturbed, and thrilled.

"I never thought that of you; and you a married man. I think I must go back into the hotel now."

"No, no, Sally, sit here a while," Don said nervously. "I'm not trying to make love to you. It's just—well—I don't know—I don't know how to say it. You know I've been working like the devil for the last two years, cooped up in an office in the city; and last year I was around with my wife's family all the time when I had two weeks' vacation. It's just this atmosphere; it's so free. And your kiddishness, and your expectancy. I feel like an older brother, that's it. I feel affectionate. You're something that I've lost, or never had."

"You needn't go on so hard. I'm not afraid of you; even if I thought you were trying to be nasty I can take care of myself. But if anybody saw you do that they would talk like everything."

"I know. Hell. Can't we ever have just an affectionate impulse without people thinking it's got some bad meaning. I'd like to put my arms about you, protect you, just from growing up and knowing what you'll have to know about what isn't."

Sally got up. "We had better go into the hotel now. You'll make me feel sad if we stay out here. Don't I see what becomes of people—my older brothers and sisters—O, I wish I could go away somewhere right now."

Don held Sally by the arm for a moment before letting her go,

149

and then he said "Yes, we'll go in. Not the first dance but a little later you'll dance with me again, won't you? You're more sensible than I am."

Sally laughed reflectively. "You were just like my oldest brother for a moment then. I do like you, so much, and it's maddening that people think that it's anything more than like, because I never would let men be familiar with me the way some of the girls I know do. But don't sit out here alone looking gloomy." Quickly Sally leaned forward and kissed Don, and then before going on into the hotel to dance, as she left him she added, "I feel like wanting to protect you too; but people just can't protect each other really."

At four o'clock in the morning there was another gathering of young men in the tent, but this time a quieter one as many of the men had retired, or had not yet come in from rowing on the lake. Peter Reynalds, Lloyd Scott, Glenn Warden, and Don Reeves only were there, for an hour's time.

"Hell," Peter Reynalds exploded, "I feel restless, and gloomy as the devil tonight. Chautauqua will be over in a few days, and that means I'll have to take to working out in the harvest fields, on some damned Swede's farm. It's what I came to town for, to earn some money if I'm going back to college in the fall."

"Whatcha throwing off on us for?" Lloyd Scott said dryly. "My girl's across the lake with Tennessee; I'm no joybird tonight myself. And the old man is insisting that I take up law. Hell, I don't want to be a lawyer, but what can I tell him?"

"That means five years more of college for you; you should worry if your old man supplies the money, and he has it," Don Reeves told him. "Don't you get in a hurry to get out of school; you'll have enough being out when you are out."

"What a joyfest," Glenn Warden said. "I've got 'em too. I was thinking tonight as I was dressing I'd like to have myself put on an operating table and overhauled. Teeth pulled out to see if there is any pus underneath that's giving me any of these new diseases; tonsils taken out; appendix removed; belly scraped; balls examined to see if they are undersized or oversized; eyes removed and polished; nose poked into to see if the bones aren't too large; and a few other cavities in me explored. I'd just like to know that my system and organs and digestion are operating right so's I'd know how much to blame on my physical condition."

"Christ, your physical condition is all right. It's people; it's the social condition," Peter Reynalds started.

"Ah dry up Pete, you always were an anarchist," Lloyd Scott interrupted him.

"Where do you get that stuff? I can have my say. What to hell? I don't notice you going around singing merrily."

"What we ought all to do is beat it to France and get into the war," Glenn Warden advised.

"Tuh, tuh. We'll be in it soon enough. America can't keep out, and I'm not wanting any army life. What would we fight for?"

"Against them damned Germans; if they win and start coming over here—" Lloyd Scott responded.

"Can it, Lloyd, can it. You'll be giving us a speech on right and justice if we don't stop you. It isn't the Germans any more than it's anybody else. Politics all over are rotten; capital, and economics; nothing else."

"Your attitudes are damned near seditious, you know," Lloyd answered with severity in his tones.

"No, son, they ain't. Not even that. They're hopeless about that kind of thing. I'm no patriot, because I can't see that one race or nation is any better or worse, or more loaded up with damn fool human beings than any other. And I can't say I expect much of any war, or social system, or political idea, going. So you've got me licked at once if you want it. I haven't any convictions, and by God, I distrust most people who have them. I just wonder what axe it is they're grinding. If there wasn't property; if there wasn't religion, particularly Christianity, and if there wasn't morality based on property and sex—"

"What are you talking about? You're dotty. We have to believe in something. What have we to stand on otherwise?"

"The ground; on instincts as education lets us retain them; the gilt-edged golden rule decorated with daisies and hung up at the foot of the bed so we can wake up in the morning with the taste of glue in our mouths and read 'God is Love.'"

"You would try to be intellectual. I hadn't realized until the last day or so what a highbrow you'd tried to become since you have been in college and away from the old town the last few years. Is that the bunk they teach you at Minnesota?"

"No, beloved; they don't teach that in colleges. I thought it. Russian literature helped me maybe, though God knows I'm off the Russians now; just as I'm off the wise weeklies. What's got me is, I know I'll have to go to war within a year because we'll be dragged into that scrap."

"You can stay out if we get in, if you will be that yellow-livered. There'll never be conscription in this country."

"Won't there? Don't you ever believe there won't. But even if there weren't I'd have to go. Not because I couldn't stand the gaff of being called yellow-livered, but just because feeling it all about me, and getting fed up with life anyway, I'd conclude what to hell, and enlist someday, but without at all believing I was going to serve any right cause by it, or that if we won that there would be a great and gentle democracy throughout the world. I'd just go, and kill Germans like the rest, because I'd get used to it being done; but if I ever stopped to think I would think that maybe some of the guys I killed were a hell of a lot more use in the world than I, or than fellows around me. But then—well, life's life. Let 'em die. What's useful anyway? Let's talk of something else. I'm stalled."

"Say, boy, if you'd use your head on making money rather than on theories, you'd be better off," Lloyd Scott advised.

"Well, at that I've made my living pretty much alone for the last five years; had to; scrapping with the old man, and he having no money anyway. You can't advise me much since you've probably never earned more than a hundred dollars in all your life; and you'll just step into a law business your old man has made for you. Maybe that'll be enough for you though."

"I won't waste my life in pessimism anyway."

"Neither will I; but I will live out my own temperament just because I must; and also because it's more interesting than letting a set of social conventions which change with every generation and with geographical situation dictate one's actions. Why limit yourself?"

"You and I don't seem to hit it off any more at all, do we Pete?" Lloyd queried.

"O yes—in a way. It's not like when we were kids, but you haven't gone away from me the way Gene Collins has; and when we were fifteen nobody existed much for either of us except the other; particularly him for me. Perhaps that's why his presence gets on my nerves now. There's something so damned stolid, and smug in him. I'll have to admit though that I can sense more sympathy in Glenn here for me, than I can in you now, whatever he feels about me. Maybe it's that you've always lived in a small town, or that you've never had to worry about making a living."

Glenn Warden answered Sam. "You're more of a rebel than I am though; but we both have Irish in us, and we get each other on that score. How is it that we never knew each other a few years back?"

"Hell—four years' difference in age. I used to see you around and thought you were a stuck-up son-of-a-gun, and that you were inclined to scorn me because I was a kid. Then you were Catholic too, and I didn't know that I wasn't even a Christian to give a damn what religion a man's family had supposedly passed on to him. About my being more of a rebel—I wonder. I think I'm just more apt to spout out what I feel.—Why call it thinking? And I'm not so well brought up. You're a gentleman of quiet melancholy, and of good manners. I'm hardly a gentleman," Peter Reynalds said.

"I'll tell you what I think, Pete, you should stick around Wentworth. You weren't meant for a city life, I can tell by the few letters you've written me. You're too nervous," Lloyd Scott spoke.

"Rot, Lloyd; there's never been a time in my life since I was four that I wasn't impatient, ecstatic one moment, morbid as hell another, and ready to be reckless almost any time. Where do you get the idea that there's peace in Wentworth? I don't know any fellows in the city who'll break loose and raise hell like a bunch of us used to back here when we got together."

"I think I'll roll into my cot," Lloyd interrupted. "Stick around as long as you want, but I'm getting sleepy. I can sleep with conversation going on, you know. You just make problems for yourself, that's all, Pete. I don't know what you're driving at half the time."

"It's this. I've got to make a living for myself, and I'm damned if there's anything I like doing that pays. I tried newspaper work; did sob stories for a while and then couldn't contemplate existence anymore; tried office work in a lumber concern and died with the boredom of companionship about me. It's the damned unrelated unrest of an Irish temperament I suppose. If the bloody war hadn't come on I'd have struck for Europe to see if living over there wasn't more gracious; aber mein gott. It's this being an American; neither a savage, nor a civilized man. A roughneck who's a little too refined. But the devil, I, for one, will let you sleep. You aren't going to let yourself suffer, old top, and I can't prove you wrong because your brain seems to work on definite things as well, or maybe better, than mine. Ta, ta. I'll head for my own tent."

Glenn Warden got up too, saying "Come on Don, let's us leave Lloyd to his slumber," and the three of them went out of the tent.

"Young Scott would be having more troubles in his mind too," Don Reeves broke into speech with, "if his old man didn't give him an allowance of about two hundred bucks a month while he's at college; and he damn well knows he doesn't have to make his way. The old man will just pass on his law business to him, and Lloyd hasn't a name for being wild in Wentworth like some other fellows have. He'll marry, and lead a calm life. He doesn't know what the grindstone is."

"Why, are you up against it too?" Peter asked him.

"Am I? For God's sake don't mention it around this burg, but my wife and I get on about as merrily as two fighting cats. She has money and she lets me know it. I'd like to ease up because as long as I make enough to live on that's enough for me, but she isn't so unambitious for me."

"Why don't you leave her?"

"The scandal—"

"To the devil with that. What do you care what the dubs who live by criticising other people think? Up and away to South America for a few years and try a pioneering life."

"I don't know. I'm thinking a number of things to do—but— well, I'm going to turn in too, fellows. See you tomorrow," Don said, and departed.

"Funny," Peter reflected aloud to Glenn Warden. "This week's gaiety at the lake seems to let us down when it begins to come to an end, doesn't it? It just lets a man know that things aren't so pretty and easy as they've seemed here, once he begins to realize he's got to get back to work."

"That's not it with me. I've enough money to live on at least. It's the fight with other people's ideas of what I ought to be, and do, that gets me; and then there are so few people I want to be with. You know I'm glad you said back in the tent that you felt a sympathy for me, because I felt reserved towards you; but I like your looks and liked them years ago when you were a kid. The only time I ever spoke to you then, you rather cut me off; thought I was patronizing you I suppose, from what you say now."

"You were, rather. It was all right too perhaps. But I remember. It was the day you said 'You won't make a football player of yourself like your older brother will you Reynalds, Jr.,' and I thought 'to hell with you,' since I knew you'd tried for the football team in high school yourself, and were perhaps trying to insinuate that I read too much. And by Lord, I liked the idea of being a precocious child in those days. I wish I could like it as well now, or that my own so-called intelligence didn't confuse me, and indicate to me that it would gain me little honour in the world. I suppose I'm ambitious for something in spite of the fact that most things known as success don't inspire me to try for them at all."

Glenn and Peter went into the latter's tent, and sat. The conversation veered to each one's detailing what he had been doing the last year or so, and what he contemplated doing in the fall. But now neither of them were as restless as they had been back in Lloyd Scott's tent, because they were not argumentative towards each other.

"Sleep here tonight," Peter invited Glenn. "Sam Hardcutt has that other cot, but he's probably sleeping with some girl down on Dub Lane tonight, and if he hasn't made the grade he can sleep on the ground. It's hot enough and he's used to it."

"All right; I feel talkative anyway, and I haven't struck anybody in the month I've been around town that I could let loose on. If a fellow can talk there doesn't seem so many problems to solve."

"At the moment I feel as if there weren't any in the universe. Why feel; why give a damn? Let everything happen as it does. You know I'm beginning to conclude that all there is to being satisfied enough is some kind of companionship, and at the right moment. That's why marriage is all off, because quite often the husband or the wife isn't the right companion at every moment, and still there's that damned tie, and comment if either wanders away a bit. I used to think it was sex, or mating, but sex doesn't solve much, and mates aren't sticking around in great numbers. I've never found one I'd take on permanently anyway."

"Companions are about as rare—"

"Have you ever got to know Sam Hardcutt? He's a good sort. Talk to him someday. He and Lloyd Scott are the only guys about town I can get on with and still think they have some sort of quality to make it work while. Lloyd's a little inclined to be dutiful, a good patriot, and to have too definite ideas about what's sensible, but he can be talked out of it. But Sam has more imagination. He and I can sit together for two hours and say nothing but grunts or a 'what to hell anyway,' or heave out a 'I don't know' or 'that's not it.' And we recognize these little grunt phrases as signifying that the mind has struck a snag, and without a spoken suggestion go on a silent hunt for hootch. Good drink solves so damned many profound, cosmic, emotional problems. There's no understanding in the universe like that silent knowing between men of the need for liquor. Christ, I think a man who can't understand why I'm bellyaching unless I give him definite reasons is an obtuse and insensitive brute."

"Well you're not that," Glenn answered him, chuckling. "We'll have to stage some intimate drunk-on parties when we get back to the city. It's too bad we didn't know each other last year when we were both in Minneapolis."

"O Lord, now you start my doubts again. I wonder. By God, after a day's work in the city—I wonder if we'll get on so well with each other there. There will, for me anyway, always be so many things I think I might like to do distracting me, and drawing me. I'm too sociable; and too anti-social. But yes, by God, we'll have a party or two anyway."

"Why do you suppose—as a change of topic—Lloyd Scott didn't make a fraternity at Wisconsin?" Glenn Warden asked.

"Ask that. Why don't half the fellows who don't? I spent a year without a friend at college, that I'd have, and then I got rushed the last month simply because I'd done theatrical criticisms for a paper and some fraternity men thought I might be worth looking over. Lloyd's too quiet. Maybe he doesn't want to be a fraternity man; I don't know. I'm shy of asking him too, and I wouldn't suggest his name to the chapter in Wisconsin because now that I'm in, I don't give a damn about the fellows that are my brothers. I stick around with older men down town, except for dances, and smokers. Why don't you do something? Write a note to men of your house there. Maybe he feels hurt a bit over not being rushed by some fraternity, because college life must mean more to him than it ever could to me."

"I might. I don't quite like him myself, but I'll take your word he has stuff, but one never knows how other fellows will take him. You've known him since you were youngsters of course, but he mayn't be good fraternity material."

"Christ yes, ten times the fraternity material I ever would be. He'd conform, and believe, and live through all the chapter's regulations. I've detested the presumption of the idea that I should cease to think, or feel, or act, in any way, except for 'the good of the chapter.' And have had contempt for the way a man up for ballot would be criticized by my brethren, whom I thought unspeakable dubs, without mind or manners or generosity. But you said I was a rebel; Lloyd isn't. He'll be a good politician someday. Dinna you worry; he'll make a name for himself. He thinks just enough to pass as a brilliant-minded young man with the dubs of the universe, but he'll never shock their sense of propriety."

The Chautauqua season went by; young people visiting Wentworth as guests, or as townspeople simply spending their vacations home from school, dispersed. The Chautauqua grounds were deserted, so that one week after the season there were no signs of the gaiety that had been except a number of rough-built summer shacks, all empty, and innumerable pop bottles, and candy boxes strewn about, with a barn of an empty hotel standing on the brow of the hill above Lake Borrows.

In Wentworth too, dullness and quiet settled, as every young person who could, managed to get out of town. The young men took jobs in the harvest fields, went on camping trips, or back to various cities; and the girls visited friends in other towns. Along the sides of Egan Avenue on some days many horses would be tied, and on Saturdays particularly, the street would be jammed with automobiles belonging to farmers in shopping for the day; but this did not alter the real lassitude which existed in the town streets for the rest of the summer. Around the drugstore a few boys loitered day and night except through meal hours; now and then a girl or so flitted down the street looking for somebody to talk to or flirt with, and generally ended by having an ice-cream soda at the confectionary store. Afternoons the town loafers lounged about the pool-hall to smoke and converse in an effort to lazily imagine some means of amusing themselves. Nothing however could be expected to take place until the school year commenced, though suggestions of setting some school house, or church, on fire, for excitement were facetiously made. So the school season was looked forward to and discussed. Then the consequent influx of new girls coming into town to attend the Normal School would present opportunities for dancing, and queening. The football season too would be on, furnishing an inexhaustible topic of conversation through the re-playing in talk of all spectacular or near-spectacular plays made by football heroes.

The school term began at Central High School; three days later the Normal School opened. This year meant the renewal of the former feudal rivalry between the two schools, a rivalry which had lapsed for some years because the students at the Normal had been a lifeless sort for a period. Now however the students at both schools were a lively, joy-loving kind, with little desire to study, and no interests apparently but to have a good time, recklessly. There were no men worth attention attending the Normal School, but this season brought a number of girls from out of town who rapidly became rivals of the most beautiful and sought-after of the regular town girls.

Class scraps began to take place at the high school too; the freshmen and sophomores were deadly enemies; the juniors and seniors were more experienced and more insistently antagonistic to each other. Whenever any of the classes gave a party, members of the enemy class tried to break it up, and, if it was given in the high school building, as generally happened, would sneak into the building to steal refreshments. Climbing in through windows on the third story of the school building, after having mounted by the fire escape, or by coming down from the roof reached by climbing a telephone pole or tree near the building, the marauders would slip quietly into the smaller room where the cakes, ice cream and punch were kept, as games were being played by the other class in a larger room. Immediately members of the other class became aware of the depredation, there would be a rush to capture the robbers, and a scrambling, running fight, that led the members of the two classes for blocks surrounding the building, ensued. Supt. May tried to assert his authority and prevent these rows, which he declared disgraceful, and a training in dishonesty and disrespect for private property, but his lectures were of no avail. At one party, he, having captured a young man by the coattail, was attacked and thrown by three others, so that all could make their escape without identity. Class rivalry was overlooked when it was a case of student against Prof. May.

School picnics, barbecue parties, dances, and when cold weather and snow came on, sleighriding parties in hayracks, began to take place too, and these occasions afforded many opportunities for sly lovemaking, and giggling amorousness. It became quite a fetish amongst the high school boys to have girls from the Normal School, thus piqueing the young town ladies. The consequences of this were an increase in the jealousy of town girls towards Normal School girls, few of whom were ever spoken to or recognized by town girls.

Hallow'een approached, and parties were planned for the evening, though it was a sure thing that few boys or young men would attend these parties, except possibly for a few minutes, long enough to partake of food and drink. The drinking of punch and the playing of kissing games were not for such a night. A handout of chow could be considered.

The night being traditionally recognized as one for mischief-making, the town board had employed a number of special policemen to guard public buildings as much as possible, and orders were posted that full penalty would be paid by any lawbreakers caught in the act on this night as on other nights. Mayor Johnson swore that there was going to be an end to the kind of rowdy ruffianism, house-breaking and property-destroying exploits that had taken place (he in those then young years aiding) in Wentworth upon this night in times past.

By nine o'clock at night men and boys began to assemble in groups of various ages, and discussion as to plans for the night's depredations took place. Naturally, citizens who had in somewise made themselves unpopular were the most surely selected victims. Public buildings, schools, churches, and the town hall were also talked about as possible to decorate in a bizarre manner. At ten-thirty after a few tricks had been performed—tricks such as pushing over privies, letting cows into cornfields, hauling wagons some distance from their owner's residence so as to cause search for them—the various groups of men and boys began to congregate in one large group. There were amongst the groups boys from nine to fifteen; young men from eighteen to thirty; and even older men of thirty-five years or thereabouts, these being toughs from the round-house and off railroad jobs mainly. There were even two men of nearly fifty participating in the night's doings, thus to prove themselves still but boys at heart.

The street back of Egan Avenue seemed by some kind of instinctive consent to have become the common meeting ground for all groups, which comprised not only townsmen and boys, but also young men from the surrounding farm country for miles around. By the time there had been arguments back and forth for three quarters of an hour, nearly two hundred beings had collected, and were scattered along in a two-block space of streetway. At last someone organized a lined up parade that lasted for but a few minutes as it marched up and down the street, first in order, then breaking into a whooping gyralating snakedance, and finally ending in confusion, with all the moil and grind of a cattle stampede. Now the night's serious business began in earnest. Plans which had been discussed amongst individuals for days before Hallow'een were put into execution. The bell clappers from every church and school in town were stolen; these were thrown into the town creek in some cases, and hidden in backhouses in others, or in one case, thrown down the hole of a privy by an older drunken man.

Tar was poured upon the steps at both entrances to the Central High School, and in sufficient quantity so that it poured out upon the walk, making it necessary the next day for boards to be laid across it to allow students and instructors to enter the building. Before the entrance of the high school, too, was placed, across the steps, a much bemired privy, odoriferous with human excrement. It took twenty men to get it there, some of the men carrying it, some advising them how to carry it, and others jumping about to register glee. While a group of some twenty boys were attempting to overturn a large-sized backhouse belonging to a grade school, one of them detected a man approaching whom he believed to be a special policeman. The detection took place because the tip of his lighted cigar showed through the darkness of the night. Pell-mell went all the culprits into flight at the announcement of this approach. Many of them were terrified at the thought of being caught, reported to their parents and perhaps expelled from school. The sound of feet beating after them—the feet of their co-conspirators—made them believe they were pursued.

With the coming of morning it was discovered that Deacon Pothatch's hayrack had been run into the town creek; and there it remained for some months, long after the creek had frozen over and was being used for a skating pond. Not till then did the Deacon remove it, cutting it out of the ice with malice aforethought, skaters believed, since two people skated right into the hole made in the ice, and up to their necks in freezing water.

Much discussion took place amongst the righteously indignant victimized inhabitants of the town about punishing the lawbreakers who had performed the various property-disrespecting acts, but as evidence was needed to punish any particular offender, nothing came of the discussion. So within a week all the discussion had died down until another year would re-vitalize it.

On one corner of town Deacon Pothatch had his farm of nearly one hundred acres, some twenty of which were taken up with apple and plum trees. In his cornfield too he also raised pumpkins, watermelons (an experimental crop), canteloupe, and gourds. To

the side of the cornfield was a large potato patch that by this season
of the year however had been harvested, as had most of the other
crops, of fruit, melon, and corn. All during the early and late fall
months he had been vigilantly attempting to protect his crops from
robberies on the part of boys and young men about town. A savage
dog which he owned had been poisoned; revile as he might the
morals of all the youth of Wentworth he was yet at their mercy, and
made himself increasingly a favorite victim of theirs because of his
tighthandedness, interfering presbyterianisms, and wrath. Several
times he'd tried peppering fruit stealers he'd detected on his do-
mains with buckshot, but this procedure, while making invaders
more cautious, but served to make it more of a game to steal from
the Deacon, or to taunt him in some way.

Stored in an outhouse not far from the Deacon's house were
many barrels of apples; a goodly number of pumpkins, and squash;
and over two hundred bushels of potatoes. Late in November it
was decided at the high school, amongst the more select of the
various classes, to have a winter picnic, which had nothing to do
with school classes. It was to be an exclusive affair; such people as
were to be in on it were to be in on it by special invitation of the
organizing group. This even meant that a number of girls from the
Normal School were to be in it, since they were the charmers
occupying the attentions of several of the high school boys organizing the picnic.

The evening of the picnic was decided upon, and a hayrack
rented to convey the thirty young people who were to be in on the
party, which would drive out to Lake Borrows on Saturday afternoon, two days after Thanksgiving, and such as could, would stay
over the week end in various cottages belonging to the parents of
some of the participants. Necessarily provisions would be needed
and these were to be supplied by the girls. However, Walter Scott,
Lloyd's younger brother, and a shade wilder, had the bright idea
that roasted potatoes and roasted squash, served with butter and
salt and pepper upon them while they were still piping hot, would
make a dish de luxe. And surely no apples could taste so good as

those stolen from Deacon Pothatch. This idea took universally with both sexes, as the exclusiveness of the party consisted in having selected only such young people as were steppers, live wires, and dead game sports. Sally Hardcutt, who attended Sunday School and Christian Endeavor regularly—because her mother made her, though the Deacon was not aware of this—said she'd be delighted to act as decoy. The Deacon had always treated her with almost too much gallantry, thinking her a right down purty gal and church inclined. She arranged to go with Vera Granger to call on the Deacon one night, purportedly to get his permission to use his town lot as a basketball ground for the high school girls' team to practice on.

Deacon Pothatch, in appearance the original of the Deacon of American Melodrama, met Sally and Vera in his front parlour. He was most cordial in receiving these young ladies of religious conviction and character, and who came to him in so confiding a manner to ask a favour. As the two young ladies conversed with him about the program it would be so nice to have at Sunday School on Christmas Eve, ten boys were pushing two barrels of apples out of the shed back of his house. These, Bill Hardcutt and Walter Scott received and hoisted upon a wagon which Buck La Brec had procured. Buck, because of his football abilities, and in spite of his family, was completely accepted by the most select of this generation of high schoolers. In fact he brought about the acceptance of his sister Katy also, though she helped herself by being the captain of the girls' basketball team.

While the two men had procured the barrels of apples, six other boys, amongst them Gerald Carlson, a Swedish contractor's son, were each making trips back and forth collecting bags of potatoes, squash, and a pumpkin or so, on the chance that some one of the girls might know how to make pumpkin pie.

The next day Deacon Pothatch was furiously upon the trail of robbers who'd filched his stored produce. He had no suspicions that school students had anything to do with it. So large a robbery had been executed by an organized gang of thieves who were marketing his produce. The Fords, the Higgins, were suspected. He inquired into the activities of some of the ruffians who hung out at the roundhouse; but all his research came to naught, for the night before the goods had been driven out to Lake Borrows and there they rested secure under lock and key until removed to feed hungry young picnickers two evenings later. Weenies were toasted over the fire; whole squash were roasted under the hot ashes, and several fires were burning which contained roasting potatoes. Coffee was boiled in large-sized tins, and the party went on boisterously, with all sworn not to reveal the Deacon episode however they might be pressed by questioning.

Walter Scott, brought up by a rigid mother, though not so carefully brought up as Lloyd had been since he was the last of five children and her eye was dimming, still had a touch of conscience. "We did take a lot of money's worth of stuff off that old man," he said.

"Heavens, Walter, don't start that," the religiously instructed Sally Hardcutt broke in. "That old man has made piles of money pinching high rents from poor families that live in his tiny cottages; and years back when everybody was hard up because of famine years here, he beat a good many people, driven by need, out of their farms. We don't need to respect property gotten as crookedly as he got his, and he pretending to be a good Christian himself."

"Well, Sally," Walter argued, "you go to church yourself a lot. Maybe there's more than one hypocrite in town."

"Shucks, your little jab doesn't phase me, Walter. Any one of you here darn well know I don't pretend to be goody. I go simply because there's a row every Sunday if I don't go, and mother says I obey her, or out I go and make my own living. Well, if she insists on the pretense for me I can carry it out long enough to be able to earn my own living."

"But you believe in church, don't you?"

"I don't know what I believe in. If you start me wondering about that, the Lord knows where I'll end with thinking. It all sounds pretty on the Sunday School cards, but tra la—let's have another hot dog, Wally, and not have an argument."

"Damn right you are, Sally," Buck La Brec said. "We'll show that old skinflint that he can't shoot buckshot at us, I guess, won't we? Do you know the old son of a b—— bite-your-finger-off charged my old man more for a barrel of apples than they charge in the grocery store, though my old man was too careless to find that out till afterwards."

It was eleven o'clock before the party split up into smaller groups and couples; and the next day there was still a semblance of festivity left in the group, but by four o'clock in the afternoon, it being chilly sleeping in the cottages at night without enough blankets, they were all ready to head back for town. So they started off, shouting, singing, bouncing about, climbing out of the rack to snowball each other, and finally climbing back in to cuddle each other. Evenings such as these were always potent for breaking up and starting romances, since the freedom of the group broke down restraint between all individuals, and adorations formerly held from afar were permitted to close in. Try as he did, however, Buck La Brec found it impossible for him to make much headway with Sally Hardcutt, who finally informed him that he musn't think he could fuss with her the way he did with Pearl Bates, the daughter of a waitress at Jack's Restaurant. No sooner had Buck moved away than Sally called Walter Scott over to talk to her. "I have it in for you," she commenced on him, "making that crack at me about my being a hypocrite."

In Walter's resulting apology and explanation he found it necessary to put his arm about Sally to console her, and she wisely whispered, "I know you won't get too fresh, Walter, but for heaven's sake try not to let Buck La Brec see you. He drives me wild with trying to make dates with me. I can't stand him. He just will talk football all the time, as though that were the only thing there is. Heavens, but I hope I can get away from this one-horse tank-town next year, and go to college where people are different from most of those here. Nothing ever happens, does it?"

The next summer the village was for a moment surprised when Glenn Warden began to go about with Lenore Thompson on his visit to town for his summer vacation. They'd stopped thinking that he would marry Mabel, but it seemed strange that he should add to her disappointed expectations the chagrin of seeing him about with her younger sister. But by the time he married Lenore, six months later, townspeople had prepared their minds not to be surprised by the event. He was not seen in Wentworth for several years after this, as business with a brokerage concern kept him occupied in Minneapolis, and he and Lenore vacationed elsewhere. Only at his mother's funeral, five years later, was he seen again, and by this time the Warden family had been well nigh forgotten by townsmen. Mary Warden, at thirty-three, had married Sam Hardcutt, who was at least eight years her junior, but a few months after Glenn's marriage to Lenore; and Glenn had helped Sam to get a position with a grain brokerage firm in Minneapolis, though Mary's inheritance was sufficient that they could have travelled had Sam not insisted upon being independent.

The waves of generations in Wentworth were overlapping each other, and the flow of new blood into town was increasing. Inhabitants came in from the country; the city limits were extended a mile beyond where they had been when Eugene Collins and Peter Reynalds were boys. Eva Downing, once so gay, and so much in evidence about town, had settled into maternity and had three children by the older Colton boy. She was about with women years her senior, all matrons. Her older sister, unmarried, was still trying to keep up an appearance of youth by being about with people many years younger than herself. Sally Hardcutt was married to Don Reeves, after having lived with him for a year, until his wife having divorced him, he was able to marry her. This had happened far away from Wentworth however, so that only rumours of it drifted back, with other rumours that Don and Sally led a very wild life in Chicago.

Lloyd Scott, whose father had died unexpectedly the year he finished the University of Wisconsin, was located in Wentworth as an attorney, but other young attorneys had come into town, so that his father's business did not pass so easily into his hands as had been expected. Eugene Collins was a Captain in the Army, after having finished West Point, and was at the moment located in Washington; it was surmised that marriage with the wealthy daughter of a United States Congressman had given him enough of a start so that he would become quite a figure in the army someday. Peter Reynalds, if remembered or mentioned at all by any of the old-time younger people, was thought to be leading a dissolute life, somewhere in Europe, probably Paris, which was known to be a horribly immoral city. He always had been fast anyway; a great drinker, and forever on the verge of being involved in some scandal or other with Normal School girls.

Yes, the waves of generations were still beating the boundary lines of the village further back into the country; and many names familiar to the town for fifteen years were spoken carelessly because some of the most promising of the young men and women of the earlier generations were clerking in the shoe or department stores, or were travelling salesmen, or schoolteachers; but the history of the village to be reported, much as history was repeating itself, would need a new collection of names, even to record the older townspeople, the tradesmen, the professional men, the church-men, the paupers and the drunkards. For old Ike Sorenson was getting so old that he couldn't get to town often now, and certainly not for a weekly drunk-on, even had there not been prohibition. He was depending entirely upon his home-made methigulum, and his silage alcohol—and a wonder it hadn't killed him ages back. His trips to town had become less frequent three years before this time, when Mrs. Simpson finally let her shack be sold and taken away from its position next to the Masonic Temple. Her gesture however was not that of defeat; she permitted it only because she too was getting too old for a seamstress, and more still because her son Brick—now Ernest—had a good position as house contractor in Fargo, and Mrs. Simpson went to live with him, declaring that "Ernie is a goot poy. He ain't stugk oop pecause his mudder is a damn crazy fool. Ve vil lif a stylish life in Fargo."

Wentworth was going on; and if it wasn't changing so much as it seemed to people who visited it after years of absence, it was expanding, and the country about was becoming increasingly farmed by a better financed type of settler than formerly. Rabbits were getting scarcer; a lone wolf, let alone a pack of wolves, had not been seen about or heard of in the community, for years. Fifty miles away the Indian reservation's population was on the decrease, as the race was degenerating with disease, and with being a dependent race. Hunting laws now had to be enforced if the county about was to keep stocked with game; forest preserves would need to be thought of if the community was to learn from the experiences of older communities. And certainly there had not been any such blizzardy and tearingly cold winter for years as that winter—was it 1902 or 1903?—when everybody but the wealthiest people had to burn cowchips to keep warmth in their houses.

Wentworth was going on; inhabitants were coming in; young people were going away, to college, to work in cities, to return disappointed, or not to return, in which case they were to be forgotten.

Carrie La Brec, née Colton, sat upon the veranda of her bungalow, swinging a little hammock, and crooning to her baby that lay within it.

bye baby bunting
papa's gone a hunting
to get a little rabbit skin
to wrap his baby bunting in.

Carrie did not sing the song long however, and when she stopped and arose, she called into her husband, Buck, "Hurry up, Buck, if we are to get any dances. Mrs. Holthausen says she will stay with the baby till twelve o'clock, but we can't expect her to stay up all night while we dance when she's had about ten kids of her own to bring up."

The sound of Carrie's voice awakened the baby in the hammock, and it began to cry with great decision. Wentworth was going on. A new generation of unrest was joining into the mainstream onflowing.

Down Egan Avenue, in a pool of shadow and light, cast by trees, and the large street arc-lamp near Mr. Jameson's house, Terrence Anderson could be seen, leaning listlessly against a tree. He was a problem. Of course nobody cared to speak to his family about him, but really he ought to have been put into an asylum long ago. You can never know when an imbecile like him might become dangerous. There was that idiot Warden, for instance, who used to be such a problem as his family was a wealthy and influential one. Of course he'd never actually done anything, but several times he had frightened little boys, and he was known to torture puppies simply out of some idiotic degenerate impulse. Someone really ought to insist that Terrence Anderson be supervised; there should be regulations about letting imbeciles wander about alone; if only somebody would speak up and tell the Anderson family about it.